ALSO BY WILL HOBBS

WILL HOBBS

NEVER SAY DIE

HARPER

An Imprint of HarperCollinsPublishers

Library of Congress Cataloging-in-Publication Data
Hobbs, Will.
    Never say die / by Will Hobbs. — 1st ed.
        p.   cm.
    Summary: When fifteen-year-old Nick Thrasher agrees to join
the photographer-brother he has never met on a journey down a
remote Arctic river, their search for migrating caribou turns into a
struggle with the elements and a fearsome bear that is part polar bear,
part grizzly.
    ISBN 978-0-06-170878-7 (trade bdg.)
    ISBN 978-0-06-170879-4 (lib. bdg.)
    [1. Adventure and adventurers—Fiction.   2. Survival—
Fiction.   3. Inuit—Fiction.   4. Climate change—Fiction.
5. Caribou—Fiction.   6. Bears—Fiction.   7. Canada—Fiction.
8. Aklavik (N.W.T.)—Fiction.]   I. Title.
PZ7.H6524Nev 2012   2011053289
[Fic]—dc23   CIP
                                                                AC

Typography by Andrea Vandergrift
13 14 15 16   CG/RRDH   10 9 8 7 6 5 4 3 2 1
❖
First Edition

to the Inuvialuit of today and tomorrow

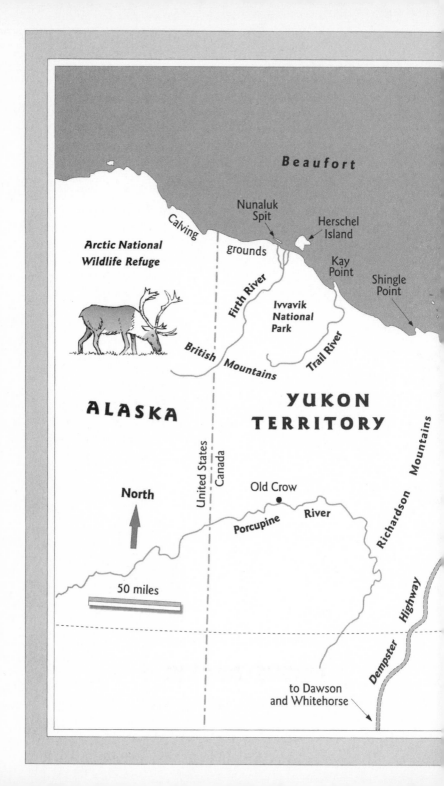

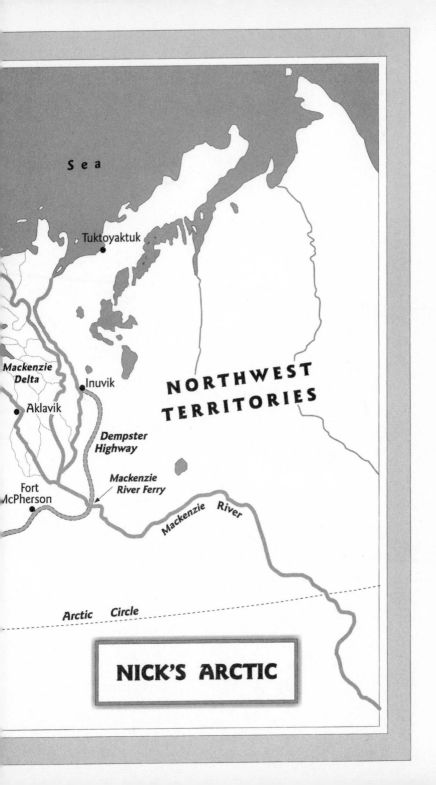

NEVER SAY DIE

1

A BEAR LIKE NO OTHER

The first weekend in May I was out on the tundra trying to get a caribou for my grampa Jonah. The odds were against me. A good flow of caribou used to come fairly close to Aklavik on their way to the calving grounds, but that was before my time. At fifteen, I was raised in the new normal. Just about everything we hunt is harder to come by.

It takes time to spot caribou. The treeless land up here in the Arctic is vast and seemingly empty. You can't get discouraged. There might be caribou over the next rise.

My second day out I finally had some luck. What I saw through Jonah's high-powered binoculars wasn't a river of caribou, not even a stream, just a trickle. Forty or so were dropping down a snowbank onto the greening tundra. Nearly half were mature cows, some with antlers and some without. The rest were yearlings and two-year-olds, including some good-sized bulls.

I stalked them for most of an hour. At four hundred yards, shielded by a knee-high boulder, I waited on my belly. The barrel of my rifle lay in a slot on the rock where it would remain dead still at the moment of truth.

As the caribou drew closer I heard the clicking of their foot tendons. *Patience*, I heard Jonah saying. *Wait for the sure thing. The last thing you want is for an animal to suffer and die far away in the brush.*

Abreast of me, fewer than two hundred yards away, the caribou stopped to graze. Some of the yearlings seized the opportunity to prance and play. The two-year-olds were grazing nonstop. The mature cows mostly kept their heads up, watching for danger. They couldn't catch a whiff of me; the wind was out of the north, off the sea ice.

I picked out a good-sized bull standing broadside to me at the very back of the group. His head was up, and he was standing still as a statue. With the crosshairs of my scope on the killing spot behind his shoulder, I squeezed off the shot.

The bullet took the young bull's life before he heard it coming. Confused and indecisive, the others milled around for a few seconds. Before I got to my feet, the leaders bolted. The whole bunch took off running at full speed.

I bled the caribou as soon as I reached him, then got to work skinning and field-dressing the bull the way Jonah had taught me. I smiled to hear my grandfather's voice, same as if he was at my side: *The sooner you let the heat out of the meat, the more tender and delicious it will be.*

I opened up the underside of the animal and pulled the innards onto the tundra. The heart, liver, and kidneys were headed home to Aklavik with care. Jonah was as traditional as they come, and had always prized the organ meat. Sick as he was now from the stomach cancer, they were the only parts of this caribou he would be able to digest.

It used to be, elders who were dying were honored with meat from an unborn calf, which is said to be tender beyond belief. I guess it still happens some, but Jonah wouldn't want me to kill a cow on his account. In the last ten years, the Porcupine River caribou herd has shrunk by as much as half, if you believe the experts. We're hoping it's not that bad, but who knows? The last couple years I've been killing only bulls, ever since

Jonah said we should stop taking cows.

The butchering went quickly. You better believe I was keeping my eye out for bears as I placed the meat inside the game bags.

Before long a pair of ravens appeared. After a couple of flybys, they landed and hopped to within ten feet, big and shiny black. I tossed them some scraps.

I had to be extra wary now. Wolves and bears watch what the ravens are up to, and know it's worth their while to investigate when the birds come to ground. It wasn't wolves I was concerned about. They would keep out of range of my rifle until I was gone. Barren-ground grizzlies are so unpredictable, you just never know.

Soon as I was done tying down my two game bags full of meat to the pack frame I'd brought along, I was ready to head back to the river and home. The ravens hopped to the gut pile as I was struggling to get that load of meat onto my shoulders.

Even the year before, I couldn't have done what I was about to do—walk three miles under that heavy a load. In the last year and a half I had put on ten or twelve pounds of muscle. I'd also shot up three inches, making me the tallest kid in school when I was only a sophomore.

Other than giving me an advantage when it came to basketball, getting tall was the last thing I would've wanted. We Inuit—a lot of people still call us Eskimos—aren't known for our height. My problem is, only half of my genes are Inuit.

I didn't really think I could make it all the way to the boat in one push. It was midafternoon, though, and I was anxious to get home. I kept going until I had the river in sight. At last I was weaving my way down the long sloping riverbank through the spindly spruce trees. My eyes were on the shore and the big motorboat.

I was half a minute from the boat when it happened. Careful not to trip as I navigated the brush, I heard something, maybe the snap of a twig, then a sudden *woosh* of breath from behind. With a glance over my shoulder I saw an enormous bear. It froze in a predatory crouch, like a lynx stalking a snowshoe hare.

This bear was more than strange. Most of its body was white like a polar bear, but its head and legs were shades of brown, like a grizzly.

The bear was close. I mean, it was right there. I had my rifle only half raised before I realized I didn't have time to shoot. The beast rushed me with a roar. All I had time to do was turn my back to it.

The impact felt like I'd been hit by a tumbling boulder. My rifle went flying as I went to the ground. I felt the claws rake my shoulder as the bear tore the pack from my back. I knew I had to get to the boat, and fast, but I couldn't move. I couldn't even breathe. The bear was standing over me, roaring and growling, big as any polar bear I'd ever seen, and I've seen four.

This animal wasn't a polar bear and it wasn't a grizzly. It was a bear like no other, some kind of monstrosity. As desperate as I was to get up, I still couldn't. Suddenly I knew what was wrong. I'd had the wind knocked out of me.

The monster was still standing on its hind legs, roaring and clawing the air.

If the creature had come down on me, it would've killed me or mauled me within an inch of my life. Instead, it swung away toward the pack loaded with meat. Carrying the whole thing in the bite of its jaws, the beast moved off with its prize about thirty feet before dropping it. Seconds was all it took for the bear to slash and bite through the rope and rip the bags open.

The raw meat had the animal in a frenzy. It stood over the meat and roared at me as if I was a threat.

Me, I was still down and sucking wind without getting any into my lungs. For what good it would do me, I pulled my hunting knife from its sheath at my hip. Finally that crushed feeling in my chest let go, and my lungs filled. I looked around for the rifle without any luck. It must have landed in the brush.

I got to my feet, faced the bear without looking it

in the eyes, and walked backward toward the front of the boat. Unthreatening as that might've been, I wasn't getting away with it. Up on its hind feet, the bear took a couple steps in my direction. As I turned toward the rope tethering the boat to a stunted spruce, the bear got down on all fours and charged. Fast as I could, I cut the rope, then spun to face the onslaught.

At the sight of me with that big knife raised—its blade six inches long—the bear stood to its full height and roared two, three times. I got a horribly close-up look at its canines, like yellow daggers. The stench spewing through those open jaws about knocked me down.

I'll never forget those small, amber eyes. I'd seen aggressive bears before, but never this aggressive, and this one had a predatory look in his eye.

I thought for sure the bear was about to come down on me. I intended to bury the blade of my knife in the monster's heart or die trying. Just then a raven croaked from behind the bear, and then a second raven. They were on the meat. The bear spun and charged the birds. I leaped behind the steering wheel and hit the starter. Soon as that powerful outboard fired up, I threw it into reverse and backed off the shore fast as I could.

You would think the roar of the motor would've thrown a scare into the bear, but no. The beast was so enraged and so intent on getting at me, it left the meat behind and charged down the riverbank. Plunging into the water with a tremendous splash, the crazy thing swam after the boat.

That bear was a powerful swimmer, and was closing fast. As I slammed the gearshift into forward, one huge paw was reaching out of the water to smack the boat. I opened up the throttle and sped away with a roar of my own.

2

THE BEARDED SEAL

I motored upstream running full out. What a relief to put a bunch of miles between me and that freakish monster. For someone who thought he didn't scare easily, I took nearly the whole way back to Aklavik—almost an hour—to calm down.

Aklavik sits in a sharp bend in the west channel of the river. Our town of six hundred in the delta of the mighty Mackenzie is hemmed in by water on all sides, including the ponds and swamps at our backs. The Mackenzie spills into the Beaufort Sea—our stretch of the Arctic Ocean—only sixty miles to the north. There's no road to Aklavik unless you count the ice road in the deepest part of winter. The Canadian government calls Aklavik a hamlet, but my family says town. Jonah says a hamlet sounds like breakfast—an omelet with ham.

I tied the boat close to where my grandparents live. On my way to Jonah's I walked down the street alongside the school. The sign in front has these words, arranged like this:

MOOSE KERR
SCHOOL
AKLAVIK "NEVER SAY DIE"

Moose Kerr was the principal here for a long time. "Never Say Die" is the motto of the school and our town, but these days for me, it's much more about my grandfather. At the moment, minutes from his door, I was wiping tears from my eyes. I couldn't bear to lose Jonah, and the end was coming soon.

Battling hard to get control of my emotions, I reached for my Inuit sense of humor. "Blubber good, blubbering bad," I said with a grimace. By the time I reached his door I had pulled myself together.

My grandparents' small home was filled with the aroma of fresh-baked bannock as I walked in after shucking my boots and torn jacket in the mudroom. Jonah was happy to see me as always, his eyes playful yet penetrating. He could tell I hadn't arrived with caribou but he wasn't disappointed. My grandfather reached up for my hand with both of his, but stayed seated in his tattered recliner, where he was spending most of his time these days.

Jonah was wearing his favorite vest, the one with the image of a bull caribou on either side. Instead of jeans he was wearing light sweatpants. It was shocking how little of him there was inside his clothes. The muscles were gone from his neck and shoulders, from his torso that used to be like a diesel drum, from those arms and legs stout as driftwood timbers.

Four years into his cancer, the great man inside the withering body hadn't gone away, though, and that's what counted. For now, the grandfather who was like a father was still with me. "So good to see you, Ug-juk," I said.

Jonah laughed at the old nickname. When I was a little kid I used to touch his chin whiskers and call him by the name of the bearded seal. He liked that. Bearded seals are large and powerful. As his laughter subsided, Jonah chuckled and said, "I'm getting more like *ugjuk* all the time. Ask your grandmother. Now that it's spring, I haul out of bed and bask in the sunshine all day."

I pulled a chair close and set up the TV trays. Gramma Mary brought food and tea from the kitchen. I gulped tea and filled my face with thick slices of bannock that I slathered with Mary's mixed jam—cranberries, blueberries, and cloudberries that my family or some of the other relatives had picked for her the summer before. "Delicious," I said in her direction. Jonah nodded his agreement though he'd barely nibbled at his.

We made small talk about how early the ice had gone out this year. The river had been open since the third week of April. Even when I was young, the ice wouldn't go out until May. The ice jams hadn't gotten that bad, hardly backing up the river, no flooding at all. As we talked I ate sliced goose breast and spread goose-liver paste on another piece of bannock. A few days back, I'd shot a bunch of geese and ducks and dropped them at the relatives' and friends' on my way home.

"Good food you've been bringing around," my grandfather said. "You haven't had much sleep since breakup, I bet."

"The long days are here, Grampa. School gets out at three and I can hunt until nine. I'll catch up on sleep when the short days come back."

Jonah nodded and smiled. "That's the way, all right. I hear there's only a few guys out for caribou this spring. You see anybody else on the tundra?"

"Nope, same as yesterday."

"Makes more sense to wait until fall. You'll get plenty

then, like you always do. But tell me about your hunt today. You've always got a story for me."

"Do I ever."

"Sometimes a story is even better than meat."

"This one's a whopper but it's true. By the way, I got a caribou, but then it got away."

His thin eyebrows lifted. "Not wounded, I hope."

"No way, I dropped him clean. Nice bull, a two-year-old."

"It got away dead. Hmmm . . ."

"I lost it, would be more accurate."

My grandfather loved riddles. It didn't take him long to figure this one out. "You had bear trouble?"

"Fifty feet from the boat, with the meat in two bags on my back."

All the humor drained from his face. "A grizzly?"

"Nope."

"Polar bear?"

"Nope."

"Black bear?"

"Nope."

"Got me stumped," he said, shaking his head. "Panda bear?"

"Grampa, this is a true story I'm telling you."

"Give me a hint, Nick. I got no idea."

"Well, your first two guesses were correct."

"Hmmm . . . a grizzly and a polar bear. You ran into *two* bears, not one. There, I got it."

"Nope, there was only one bear."

"One bear that was a grizzly *and* a polar bear?"

"That's the animal—a cross between the two. Have you ever heard of such a thing?"

"Never. Tell me what it looked like."

"Light brown head of a grizzly, wide and dished-out in the forehead. The muzzle was almost white. It had the long neck of a polar bear, with the fur getting less brown and more white between head and shoulders."

"Hump of a grizzly?"

I had to think a bit. "Not hardly. And the shape of the body was longer, like a polar bear's, like it was made for swimming. The fur on the torso was white like a polar bear's, but dirty white. On its legs the fur went from white high on the haunches to dark brown below the knees."

"What a strange-looking animal!"

"I know!"

"Long claws on the front feet like a grizzly?"

I closed my eyes and remembered the bear standing above me. "I'm pretty sure the front claws were shorter, like a polar bear's. And the feet were shaggy and big as frying pans, like a polar bear's."

"Fur on the bottom of the feet?"

"Some, but not as much as a polar bear's got."

"How big was this bear?"

"Bigger than any barren-ground grizzly, big as a polar bear. Nine hundred pounds, easy, and aggressive like you wouldn't believe. Like it had no experience with humans and saw me as prey."

"Tell me what happened."

I did, from when I first saw the bear at no more than twenty feet to when I escaped in the motorboat. As he listened, Jonah never blinked once. When I was done, he said, "Nick, you were lucky to get away with your life."

"Don't I know. He came an eyelash from nailing me. What do you figure it was, Grampa?"

"A grizzly and the great white bear have mated, sounds like. Get that close, used to be, *aklak* and *nanuq* were trying to kill each other."

Grampa Jonah worried his chin whiskers. "We hear about grizzlies crossing on the sea ice to the islands up north. We hear about starving polar bears hundreds of miles south of the ocean. Now this strange new stalking bear with no fear of man. This last year since I've been too sick to go with you, I haven't worried. I was hunting on my own to feed my family when I was twelve, and you're a real good hunter. But maybe for now, with this aggressive bear in the area, you should go with one of the other hunters."

"I was thinking the same thing."

"We'll have to get the word out. It might show up in town anytime now. This is one more bad sign, Nick. Things are changing so fast, I don't know what the world is coming to. I don't even know the names of some of the birds and the insects that are showing up. The crazy winters we're getting these days, less and less sea ice, more wind and open water in summer, harder to go whaling, the caribou not showing up where they used to and not so many, more bad storms with lightning, even. We're not supposed to get lightning up—"

Jonah's voice caught and he started coughing real bad. My grandmother looked startled. I quickly poured him a cup of tea. He was able to drink a little and stop coughing.

"I'm sorry," I said. "That stuff about things changing for the worse isn't any fun to talk about."

Jonah shook his head. "Fun has nothing to do with it. It's important to talk about those things. We have to deal with whatever comes, Nick. We're just going to have to adapt, that's all. We have always adapted—that's why we're still here. It's going to be up to you and the rest of the young people."

"We'll do our best," I said, without being able to picture what that even meant. If the future didn't include enough animals to hunt, I had no idea how I would live or what I would live for.

3

A LETTER FROM ARIZONA

I made a beeline for home. The walk to my side of town took only ten minutes. My mother was away, but the rest of the family was there, my aunt Becky and my cousins Billy and Suzanne.

My mother was six hundred-some miles away in Yellowknife, the capital of the Northwest Territories, taking the classes she needed for a better nursing job at the clinic here. It was killing my mom that she couldn't be home to look in on her father every day. I knew how afraid she was that he might die while she was away.

"Any luck?" shouted Billy as I came through the door. Billy was eleven, keen on hunting, and starting to get good at it. Suzanne, two years younger, was asking the same question with her eyes, as was Aunt Becky, who was at her sewing machine working on a pair of sealskin mukluks. She sews for the Aklavik Fur Company.

"No luck," I mumbled, putting off my story until I'd eaten. My eyes went to the counter and the stove top. The dishes were already done. It was seven in the evening.

"Plenty of stew left in the pot," my aunt said cheerfully.

"Thanks. Smells great. I'll get washed up and be right back."

"Tell him about the letter," said Suzanne. She was doing homework at the kitchen table across from Billy.

I was in a hurry to take a look at my aching shoulder but there was something in Suzanne's voice that stopped me in my tracks. I get a lot of emails, but letters almost never. "What letter?" I said as casually as I could manage.

"It's not from Canada," Billy chimed in with a knowing look.

"It's from the States," my aunt explained.

"It's mysterious," added Suzanne.

As soon as I had the envelope in hand, I saw what it was that had them acting strange. The letter was addressed to Nick Powers, which used to be my name, but not for the last three years. When I was twelve I told my mother I hated the name Powers. I still remember her reaction. "What's up?" she teased. "Won't you miss the kids at school calling you Super Powers?"

"A little," I admitted. "I just can't relate to Powers. It's not who I am. I want to have your name and Jonah's. I want to be Nick Thrasher. That's who I am."

So here I was, three years later, getting a letter addressed to Nick Powers. My eyes went to the name of the person who had sent it: Ryan Powers. I'd never met Ryan Powers but I knew who he was—my much-older half brother. We had the same biological father, an American named Conrad Powers. My white DNA comes from him.

My mother and my father met by chance at Shingle Point, where most of Aklavik goes every July to escape the bugs, to fish, and to hunt beluga whales. Conrad Powers was kayaking the Northwest Passage across the top of Alaska and Canada all the way to Greenland. He was the first to ever do it in a kayak. "An adventurer" is how my mother describes him. He never came back to marry her, like he was talking about. He died climbing a mountain in the Himalayas when I was only a month old.

"Hmmm," I said, slapping the envelope against my leg. "I wonder what this is about."

Inside the bathroom, I set the letter aside and took a look at my shoulder. I'd gotten off with a couple of welts.

Just to be safe, I scrubbed the welts with soap and sterilized them with rubbing alcohol. My eyes kept going to the envelope. The return address was Flagstaff, Arizona. I already knew my half brother lived there. When I was born he was thirteen years old. These days my white brother would be . . . twenty-eight.

I used to check out his website when I was younger, but I hadn't been on it since I changed my name. I made myself get over my curiosity about him.

I was dragging my feet about opening that envelope. "Later," I mumbled, "after I eat dinner." It's not like I wasn't curious to find out what the letter was about. It's just that I didn't want to react like this was a huge big deal.

Why, I wondered, was my brother getting in touch now, when he never had before, back when I was always hoping he would? I used to imagine he would take me on his raft through the Grand Canyon. Maybe that's what the letter was about, now that I was old enough to do something like that.

I couldn't resist opening it before going to bed. Big mistake. Between my brother and that awful bear, I ended up tossing and turning all night. Soon as I got up next morning I picked up the letter and reread it. Here's what it said:

Dear Nick,
Hello up there at the roof of the world. I should begin by telling you how many times I've meant

to get in touch, or better yet look you up so we could meet in person, get to know each other, maybe spend some time together. Sorry to say, I never got it done.

Here's what I'm writing about. I'm going to be close to Aklavik next month. I'm going to drive my pickup all the way from Flagstaff, Arizona, where I live, to Whitehorse, then on to Dawson City and all the way up the Dempster Highway to Inuvik.

I'm going to be right across the delta from where you live—if you're still there—so I could arrange to fly over to Aklavik. That would be great, but if you happen to be in Inuvik, that's another possibility.

Before I go any further I should fill you in on myself and what I'm up to. The last four years I've been making my living as a wildlife photographer. These last two years, I've been taking pictures for National Geographic magazine. I've been able to travel to some of the most remarkable wild places left on earth and shoot truly amazing wildlife.

To backtrack a bit more, before I was a professional photographer I made my living as a raft guide rowing people down the Colorado River through the Grand Canyon. I did that for four *years. I'm coming north in June to run the Firth River in Canada's Yukon Territory.*

From everything I've read and heard, the Firth River will put me in the best position to photograph the Porcupine caribou herd at a time and place where I have the best chance of seeing big numbers of them. Too many trees where they winter, in the Porcupine River country.

Of course I'm hoping to photograph lots of other Arctic wildlife during the same time, especially the barren-ground grizzly. I might as well cut to the chase and tell you I'm hoping you'll join me for this trip down the Firth River.

I realize this is a long shot, Nick. If you're interested, there are a few things you and your family need to know. It would be just the two of us making the trip. Normally I travel alone. Traveling with a group makes it nearly impossible to photograph wildlife. I have plenty of expertise when it comes to wilderness, white water, and medical—I'm an EMT. Still, there's always an element of danger when you're way out there, as I'm sure you know very well, living where you do. I will have a satellite phone along in case of emergency.

Talk it over with your mother, Nick. Like I

said, it's a long shot. You probably have plans for the summer. Another thing . . . this trip won't be anything like the raft trip down the Firth River that tourists take. Instead of eleven days, I'll be taking three to four weeks. You might be bored to tears. If you choose to join me, I will cover all your expenses. I have a bush plane booked for June 15.

See what you think and write me back. We can go back and forth by email if that works for you. In any case, I hope to see you next month. Please give my best to your mother. One more thing . . . I'll be writing the article as well as taking the pictures. Right now I'm thinking of the title as "Change Comes to the Arctic." I have been following the issue of climate change in the North for years now, and would greatly benefit from your outlook on the decline of the caribou and more. Looking forward to hearing from you,

Sincerely,
Your brother Ryan

4

NICK'S BEAR

School wasn't my first priority after breakfast. I headed downriver with Wayne Tetlichi, head of our Hunters and Trappers Committee, to fetch my rifle. Wayne had a camera along in hopes the bizarre bear had left prints. He was also hoping we could find scat or hair.

Wayne was Gwich'in Indian, in his forties, lean and smart as a whip. I had hunted with him a couple of times. As a tracker he had no equal. I eased back on the throttle as we approached the spot. Wayne reached for his rifle just in case the monster was still hanging around.

We went ashore, cautious as could be. Real quick, Wayne came across a set of quality tracks in the mud.

"Big 'un," Wayne said, as he handed the rifle off to me and began to take pictures of the longer footprints from the back feet and the shorter footprints from the front feet.

I could see for myself that the tracks indicated polar bear, from their size and shape and the short claws on the front feet. Grizzlies use their long claws for digging up rodents. Polar bears don't need those; they swat seals. These tracks even showed hair on the soles of the feet, another indication of polar bear.

Wayne didn't say anything, but I could pretty well guess that he was wondering if my imagination had gotten away from me. It wasn't as rare as it used to be for a polar bear to show up fifty miles south of the Arctic Ocean. Hunger and desperation had driven one nearly five hundred miles south, down toward the Great Slave Lake.

We went looking for my rifle and found it in the bushes. The bear had sent it flying about twenty feet through the air. Wayne tracked my bear a mile onto the open tundra in hopes it had left some scat. It hadn't, but when we returned to the river and discovered my shredded game bags, Wayne found strands of hair on them. To my relief, the hair was distinctly brown. "Like a grizzly's," Wayne said with a nod in my direction. "You said the head and neck fur was brown. Makes sense, the hair on these bags would be from the head or neck—probably face."

Wayne put on the latex gloves he had brought along. With the hairs zipped inside a kitchen bag, he said, "I'll get this to Roger McKeon. He'll have it tested. If this bear is something new and dangerous, people need to know."

Roger McKeon is Canada's big expert on polar bears. People up here respect Roger McKeon for what he knows but don't feel right about the way he gets that knowledge. Harassing polar bears from helicopters, shooting them from the air with tranquilizer darts so you can put a satellite collar on them and track their every movement—that isn't right. As Jonah would say, "You never mess around with wildlife."

I heard Roger McKeon talk about polar bears only six weeks before, when he came to Aklavik to meet with the high school kids. He told us he'd been collaring polar bears in the Canadian Arctic almost thirty years, and they were getting harder and harder to find even by helicopter on account of the vanishing ice. He told us that more and more polar bears are turning up drowned, especially after storms, which used to be unheard of.

"Here's how bad it's getting," McKeon told us. "Last summer, a polar bear swam nine days and four hundred and twenty-six miles across the Beaufort Sea in a desperate search for ice to haul out on. We knew *Ursus maritimus* could swim two hundred miles . . . four hundred is phenomenal. In freezing seawater, it must have taken every last ounce of her strength. Unfortunately, her two-year-old cub drowned along the way."

With a shrug and a grimace, McKeon said, "Polar bears can't survive without their platforms of ice, my friends. Neither will their prey, the ringed seal. Without doubt, the planet is warming, and the climate is changing almost everywhere. Where it's changing the fastest is in the Arctic. In your lifetimes, the polar bear will probably go extinct in the wild. Think about that when you choose to take Aklavik's quota. That's all I'm asking. The choice will be yours."

McKeon left the gym with a scattering of applause, mostly from the teachers. The rest of us didn't know how to react. If there's one thing the people of the Arctic don't like, it's people from the south telling us "the right thing to do." Polar bears have been part of our diet since forever.

Back in town, Wayne headed for the post office and I headed for school. With testing behind us and only a few weeks to go, we were having a lot of assemblies. I walked into the middle of one about employment in the mining industry. I can't say I paid good attention to the people from the Diavik Diamond Mine or the pictures they were showing. I had two years before I graduated high school. I wasn't excited about working hundreds of miles from home in a giant pit, or on an offshore oil platform when the government gave the green light to the oil companies to go after their discoveries under the Beaufort Sea.

Mostly I wasn't paying attention because my mind was on that letter from my half brother. It was exciting to hear from him, but at the same time I was resentful that he had waited this long, like I didn't exist. At the end of the letter, when he said he wanted to find out what I thought about climate change and the decline of the caribou, it seemed like a clue that his invitation was more about his article than it was about me.

This line of thinking had me disappointed with myself for being so small-minded. Ryan had said it was a chance for us to get to know each other. And the offer he was making was generous and incredible, a once-in-a-lifetime opportunity. As I first read the letter, the name of the river he was going to run really jumped out at me. Jonah had been telling me about the Firth River since I was a little kid. "A hunter's paradise," my grandfather called it. He hadn't been back since he was a young man, but whenever he told stories about it, his memories were keen as yesterday.

The assembly was coming to a close and so was the back-and-forth in my head. Here's what I knew for sure: even if I wanted to go on the trip, there was no way I would do it, not while Jonah was dying. I needed to stay and be with him, and say good-bye when the time came.

A couple of days went by with me not answering the letter. It wasn't like I had to do it right away.

Meanwhile, Aklavik was on alert for "Nick Thrasher's bear," as it was being called. At school, having to tell my story over and over again was getting old fast. Hearing "Nick's bear" made my skin crawl. People from Aklavik are not out to get attention. The hunters who have the most to brag about never do.

I got an email from my mother. She asked what was up with the letter from my brother. Aunt Becky mentioned to her that I had gotten it but hadn't wanted to talk about it. Which was true. All I said was, it's something I need to think about, and please don't say anything about it to the grandparents. I wanted to spare Jonah from having to think about what I should do about my brother and his invitation.

By the time of my mom's email I was ready to bounce the letter off her. Rather than give her a secondhand version of what my brother had written, I faxed her the letter from the clinic with Aunt Becky's help. While I was at it,

I gave my aunt the short version of what was going on.

Soon as I faxed the letter to Yellowknife, I emailed my mother that there was no way I would go on my brother's river trip on account of Jonah.

She emailed back after she'd read the letter and my email. *I understand you wanting to stay with Jonah, but he might pass away sooner rather than later. Your brother sounds like a real expert in the outdoors, like his (your) father was. If you really want to go on the trip and have that time with him, you might think about just telling him where you stand. If it works for him to wait until he gets to Inuvik to find out if you're coming, the two of you could start talking about what the trip would be like. You could find out if it was a good fit for you.*

Thanks, Mom, I wrote back. *That's really good advice.*

A few minutes later I sent my first email to Ryan. I was really cautious about his invitation. I didn't want to act excited, even though I was. All I said was, I'm interested but can't be definite, and then I explained why.

Ryan emailed back that he was happy to be in contact with me, and he completely understood. He thought it was great that I was so close with my grandfather. He would just proceed as if I was coming, right up to when it came time to shop for groceries in Inuvik.

My mom thought Ryan's reply was pretty classy. It

showed he really wanted to get to know me and have me along.

The famous photographer sent me a checklist of the clothing he was bringing along, for me to make use of if that was helpful. He said he had rafted a river in Canada's central Arctic the summer before and knew we had to be prepared for ninety-degrees Fahrenheit and also for cold rain and snow. Any clothes I didn't have already that I might like to take along, he would be happy to buy for me in Inuvik before we flew out for the trip.

I told him I didn't have one of those bug shirts with the see-through mosquito netting in the front of the hood. *Good, I'll get you one*, Ryan wrote back. *As I found out last summer, the bugs on the tundra can get really bad.*

We were getting along pretty well on the email. The chances of me going on this trip were slim, but it felt good to be in touch with my half brother.

At school, the talk about "Nick's bear" was starting to die down. With only ten days left before we were out for the summer, there was a lot going on. I went back to living under the radar.

5

I'M NOT THERE YET

It caught me by surprise when Ryan emailed on the twenty-first of May to say he was already packing his pickup with his river gear. He was going to take two weeks for the driving trip from Arizona to Inuvik. The town of Inuvik sits forty miles east of us, on the other side of the Mackenzie River delta. It's got three thousand people and is way more modern than we are. You can actually drive to Inuvik from wherever, which is fairly incredible if you get out a map and check out its location. Other than Fort McPherson, on the road to Inuvik, there isn't another town above the Arctic Circle in all of Canada that you can drive to.

Ryan's email said he would be arriving in Inuvik

a week before flying out with a bush pilot into the Yukon Territory and the headwaters of the Firth River on June 15. He was hoping, before he got serious about shopping and the rest of what he needed to do in Inuvik, to spend about three days in Aklavik. He said he had already looked into chartering a flight to our airstrip. He'd found Daadzii Lodge on the internet, and would be staying there.

Holy smoke, I thought, he's going to come here, spend three days here, right in Aklavik?

There's only one word to describe my reaction: *dread*.

My eyes darted back to the email. He explained that it would really help him with the research he needed to do for his article if he could interview hunters in Aklavik. He was especially interested in what our hunters would have to say about climate change and the Porcupine caribou herd, and whether climate change was affecting the whaling we did from our summer encampment at Shingle Point.

I about hit the panic button. Oh great, I thought. This is just what I need. All the hunters in Aklavik looking at me like, Thanks a lot. All the kids I'd grown up with looking at me differently than they had before. I could hear them talking. "Did you know that Nick Thrasher has a brother, right here in Aklavik?" "No way, who is he?" "The white guy who flew in this morning." "What's he like?" "Just what you'd expect. He's going all around town asking people the usual dumb questions, like 'Do you hunt?'"

This much I knew right away: If my brother came to Aklavik before his river trip, whether or not I went on it with him, I was going to have to dig a very deep hole to keep from dying of embarrassment.

I emailed him right back and told him "some other time." With my grandfather dying, my family couldn't have a guest in the village, even if he was staying at Daadzii Lodge.

Ryan emailed back and said he completely understood. He was being really cool about this, said he'd spend the extra days in Inuvik instead. He was still hoping I could come on the trip.

I see your phones are just landlines in Aklavik, no cell service. Call me at the Mackenzie Hotel in Inuvik anytime in the week before the trip or leave a message. We can work out shopping details then. I honor your feelings for your grandfather. If I don't see you, here's hoping the not-too-distant future will bring us together.

I was so up and down and all over the place with my feelings. I wondered if I had made a mistake telling him he couldn't come to Aklavik. No, I still couldn't picture it.

May turned to June. School was over, the bugs were out, and the sun was up twenty-four hours a day. Ryan was on the road somewhere in his pickup with his rafting gear and camera stuff. My mother was home from Yellowknife, and Jonah was somehow still hanging on. The skin on his gaunt face was papery thin.

I was visiting my grandfather nearly every day. I told him about the fish I was catching, the birds I was shooting, the muskrats I was trapping, and the moose I'd been lucky enough to get. The bull was wading one of the countless small streams that meander through the delta. Jonah was delighted with the organ meat. He still didn't know anything about Ryan's letter and the Firth River trip he had offered me.

The head nurse at the clinic in Aklavik had recently suggested to my grandfather that he might be more comfortable, as she put it, at the new regional hospital in Inuvik. Jonah waved that off without even having to think about it. My grandfather wanted "to go to the other side," as he put it, at home in Aklavik.

With only a week to go before my brother's date with the bush pilot, my mother said maybe I should reconsider about going on the trip. "I have a feeling this trip is going to open some doors for you. Jonah will understand. I think he would want you to go."

"You're probably right about that," I said. "I just can't."

My mother gave me a hug and said she was proud of me. She told me I had been a big part of her father's life.

36

"You haven't told your brother yet that you're not going, have you?"

"Not yet," I said. "I guess I will pretty soon."

The day after that, during my visit with Jonah, after we'd been talking about some of our adventures on the sea ice, he came out of a lull in the conversation with this: "One of my biggest regrets, Nick, is that I never took you way back into the mountains up the Firth River. I was only there one time myself, a long, long time ago. But oh my, so pretty—it was something to see. Hunter's paradise. Saw so many caribou all at once, well, they covered the valley and the mountainsides far as my eyes could see."

"That was something, Grampa. I hope to see it someday."

He gave me a look and said, "I think you should, sooner rather than later."

I could tell that he knew. "Who told you?"

"Your mother."

"Hmmm . . . she wasn't supposed to."

"Well, it's hard to argue with a mother's instincts. I'm glad I found out."

"But I want to be with you. A month is way too long. . . . I'd even miss the beginning of the whaling season at the coast."

"Your mother and your aunt can run the motorboat

and open up the cabin by themselves. You can catch a ride with somebody soon as you're back."

"True, but I've been thinking anyway that my brother's trip is going to be a bust. He wants to take pictures of huge numbers of caribou, like you saw back in the day, but it's been years since anybody's seen that."

"Could still happen. If big numbers are still out there to be seen, he picked the right place to go look. He also picked the right time. The cows and their calves will be migrating east out of the calving grounds in Alaska by then, and the bulls will be joined up with them after their own migration. You never know, he might get lucky."

I reached for another excuse. "I . . . I'm not sure I even want to get to know him. He's just a stranger."

"He's also your brother. That's something special."

"I don't want to be disappointed. He's obviously an environmentalist, probably the kind who doesn't approve of us hunting whales and bears. When he talks about shooting caribou, it's with a camera. What if we don't get along?"

Jonah reached out his hand and placed it on mine. "Only one way to find out, Nick."

A tear or two escaped my eyes. "Here's how it is, Grampa. I want to be here with you till the end. Is that so wrong? I couldn't handle it way out there for a whole month. I want to be here."

He squeezed my hand hard as he could, which wasn't very hard. And he chuckled. "So that's it! That's what this is all about."

"Well, sure."

"Listen carefully, Nick. There comes a time when the caribou won't even try to run from the wolf, and the moose won't run from the bear. That's when they stand, and let death take them. They finally accept it. I'm not there yet. I've still got the fight in me. I want to hear your stories when you get back, and that will give me all the reason in the world to hang on. After that, the wolf or the bear can have me, whichever gets here first."

I couldn't help myself—tears filled my eyes, and I hugged Jonah ever so gently.

"Good," he said. "Now go."

An hour later I called up the Mackenzie Hotel in Inuvik. The lady said Ryan Powers was out of his room. Did I want to leave a message?

This was better than having to talk to him. The message I left said I would meet up with him at the hotel sometime on the fourteenth. He could go ahead and buy groceries for two.

6

THE EXPERTS ARE STUNNED

Real early on the morning of the fourteenth of June I threw my stuff into the boat—a big duffel bag, a small backpack, and my rifle in its hard plastic case. My mom stepped into the passenger seat next to me and we headed upriver. There was a lot to talk about, but the engine noise made that impossible.

At full throttle, it took hours to reach the Mackenzie River ferry at the head of the delta. I unloaded my stuff quickly. My mom and I were saying good-bye when she surprised me. "We've hardly ever talked about your father. Whenever I tried, it made you uncomfortable."

"I know," I admitted.

"Because you never wanted to think about that part of yourself."

"You're right. In my heart, I'm a hundred percent Inuit."

"You're as fine an Inuk as they come. I just wanted to say that your father was an amazing person. I've never met anybody like him before or since. Smart, kind, funny, and so full of life."

"Good, I'm glad."

"You never got to know him, but give your brother a chance, that's all I wanted to say. Don't go all silent aboriginal on him, okay?"

I cracked up. "Sure, but what if he rubs me the wrong way right off the bat?"

"If he seems like a good person, you can meet him halfway. If he doesn't, give me a call and I'll come and get you right here, tomorrow."

We said some other things, mostly about Jonah. Then we hugged and said good-bye. My mom got behind the wheel and hit the starter. With a wave she was headed downriver to join my aunt and my grandmother at Jonah's bedside.

I eyeballed the line of vehicles waiting to get on the ferry. Most of them had come 450 miles up the gravel highway from the paved highway outside of Dawson.

They were pretty well caked with mud. The tourists were staying inside their vehicles. The day was warm and buggy. Here came the ferry returning from the eastern shore of the mile-wide Mackenzie.

I walked onto the ferry, scouting each vehicle as they came aboard. Usually you can catch a ride with locals from nearby Fort McPherson who are on their way into Inuvik for the day. A Gwich'in guy helped me out. His name was James and he was on his way to a doctor's appointment. He told me to throw my stuff in the back of his truck and hop in.

The drive to Inuvik took about ninety minutes. James filled my ear with how lousy the economy was. He used to have plenty of work when the oil and gas exploration was booming, but ever since the world economy went sour in 2008, he hadn't been able to find any kind of a job. He'd had to go back to subsistence living. "If we didn't have the fall caribou hunt," he said, "we'd be in a really bad way."

"Same goes for Aklavik," I told him.

I had James drop me by the igloo-shaped church in the center of town, a few minutes' walk from the Mackenzie Hotel. It was early afternoon and the sun was blazing. I told myself that it would be cooler on the Firth River. It was time to think positive about meeting my brother.

I half expected to find Ryan waiting as I lugged my

stuff into the lobby of the hotel. He wasn't there, but had left a message. Ryan had paid for a second room for me that night. I should go ahead and move in, then look for him at Boreal Books or the office of Ivvavik National Park.

I tried the bookstore first. There was a flyer on the door with Ryan's name and the cover of his new book, *America's Grandest Wild Places.* The flyer said he would be signing and visiting from noon until two. I had missed him by fifteen minutes.

I left the bookstore and headed down Mackenzie Avenue. Through the window of the Parks Canada office I saw a tall young man talking with a short park warden in uniform. It took me a couple of seconds to identify the taller one as Ryan. He had the dark, wavy hair I remembered from his website. With the full beard he was wearing now, it was harder to see the resemblance to me.

I got all jumpy and walked away before either one noticed me looking in. I could always tell my mother and Jonah that he rubbed me the wrong way.

Well, I couldn't live with chickening out. I headed back for the Parks Canada office. Ryan and the park warden were having such an intense conversation about the poster on the wall—a big map of the Mackenzie delta—they didn't notice me slip inside. I sidled behind a partition with a display about Ivvavik National Park.

"After the Mississippi," the warden was saying, "the Mackenzie is the second-biggest river in North America."

"Here's where I took the ferry across the river."

"Correct. Downstream, here's Point Separation, where the river divides into three channels and the delta begins. The Mackenzie's delta—twelfth biggest in the world—is a hundred miles long and generally forty miles wide."

"A wonder of the world to be sure," my brother marveled. "What a maze. Thousands of islands and connecting streams, and so many lakes—any idea how many?"

"Roughly twenty-five thousand."

"Here's Aklavik! I was hoping to get there—it didn't work out. When was it first settled?"

"Early in the twentieth century during the rush for the white fur of the Arctic fox. Inuit from the coast and Indians from upriver began to settle around a new trading post. It became the biggest settlement in Canada's northwest Arctic. There were more than sixteen hundred people there in the 1950s when the government decided to shut it down. They built Inuvik to replace it."

"How come?"

"Aklavik was prone to flooding. Where we're standing right now is well above the Mackenzie's floodplain.

44

Inuvik was a modern miracle, but when the time to move came, half of the people in Aklavik said thanks but no thanks—we're staying put. What the government could never replace was their traditional subsistence way of life. That's where their motto comes from—'Never Say Die.'"

"That goes in my article for sure. I take it the hunting and fishing were better over there?"

"Yes, and Aklavik's location allowed the Inuit to keep sealing and whaling on the coast."

"I was hoping to visit their summer encampment at Shingle Point after my trip. Any chance of photographing a polar bear there?"

"Not likely—too many people. Half of Aklavik is there during July. Your chances of photographing barren-ground grizzlies during your Firth River trip are much greater. The grizzlies follow the caribou. Keep your eyes out for the hybrid of the two."

"Come again, Dave? A hybrid? Hybrid bear?"

I had been following this conversation real close as it was, but now I was all ears.

"A polar bear and a grizzly have mated," the park warden said. "The bear experts are stunned."

"Has it ever happened before?"

"A couple of times, they're saying, in zoos. Canada's polar bear expert, Roger McKeon, is guessing that the changing climate is behind the appearance of this first one in the wild. We know that grizzlies have crossed on the sea ice to some of the islands in the high Arctic—why is anybody's guess. Personally, I think the two species mated up there. It took years for the hybrid cub to grow up and find its way down here. If it was born down here where there's a lot more hunters around, it would've been noticed before it got to be full-grown."

"You said keep your eye out for the hybrid. . . . If it's alive, how are they so sure it's a cross between grizzly and polar bear?"

"They even know the gender of the parents—male grizzly, female polar bear. The DNA was from hair collected at the scene of a bear encounter that a hunter from Aklavik had on the western side of the delta last month."

"Man, would I love to interview that hunter for my article. That must've been a strange-looking bear."

"I hear the hunter was a teenager."

"What is the hybrid bear being called? They must have given it a name."

"The Canadian Wildlife Service has floated two possibilities. One is *nanulak*, the other is grolar bear. *Nanulak* is a combination of the Inuit names for the two different bears. Grolar bear, as you've already guessed, is a combination of *grizzly bear* and *polar bear*. Grolar bear is the one that seems to be catching on."

"I vote for grolar bear," I said as I stepped from behind the partition.

7

PURE FOOLISHNESS

Ryan looked confused at first—he'd never even seen a picture of me. Real quick, he broke into a big smile and called my name. He was tall—more than six feet. He strode across the room and reached out his hand for mine. His eyes were greenish, flecked with brown.

Ryan introduced me—to the park warden's surprise—as his brother, Nick Powers.

"Nick Thrasher," I corrected him.

"I didn't realize," Ryan said, and explained to the park warden that I was from Aklavik and was going to run the Firth River with him.

I wanted to hear more about the bear. I asked the park warden, whose name was Dave Curry, how long he had known about the DNA test.

"We just heard about the results late yesterday," Curry said. "They haven't been released to the press yet."

"Say, Nick," my brother said, "I wonder if you might know the teenager who had the encounter with the grolar bear. You would've heard about it. You know that kid?"

"I do," I said. "It was me."

You can imagine their faces, especially my brother's. "Could you tell it was a hybrid?"

"That looked pretty obvious."

"Could you tell us about the encounter?"

I kept it short, told it pretty flat, and left out a lot. I could tell that my brother had no end of questions but he held back. So did the park warden. I'd already told the bear biologist who came to talk to me how crazy-aggressive the bear was.

Ryan asked if I'd had lunch and I told him I hadn't. We went to the Mackenzie Hotel's restaurant. I ordered a hamburger and fries with gravy. First thing, Ryan asked about my grandfather. I said, "He's hanging on one day at a time."

"I'm sorry you're losing him, but I'm so glad you could come. Have you been in Ivvavik National Park before, over in the Yukon Territory?"

"Only on the coast, not in the mountains."

He was hoping I'd say more. When I didn't, Ryan said, "Ivvavik's remoteness is half of the appeal. It's nothing like our national parks back home. When the park office is two hours away by airplane, that tells you a lot. As I understand it, there are no communities on the entire north slope of the Yukon Territory. Not a single person lives there year-round."

Our food arrived. My hamburger beat the fast-food burgers I'd had in Inuvik after basketball games, but it didn't have the flavor of ground caribou. I went heavy on the ketchup.

My brother was a fish out of water, and didn't know where to start. At least he wasn't going to ask, "Do you hunt?"

He hesitated, then asked, "Your branch of the Inuit is called the Ee-noo-vee-al-oo-it, right?"

Close enough, I thought. I nodded my agreement as I dug into my fries.

"If I got this right, Inuit means 'the People.' What does Inuvialuit mean?"

"It's hard to translate into English. 'The Real People' is pretty close."

"Do you speak the language?"

"A little. We take it at school."

Ryan eased off on his questions and finished his sandwich. Soon as he paid the bill, we got into his pickup to go shopping. Ryan had a big cooler and three metal boxes he called "ammo cans" in the bed of the truck, all of them empty. We were going to spend the rest of the afternoon shopping for the fresh food and other stuff to fill them up.

Ryan drove us to the Northmart. It was a hot day with hardly any wind and the mosquitoes were pretty bad. It was good to get inside. We started in the clothing section. My brother bought that bug shirt for me. Next stop was sporting goods. Ryan was asking if I'd brought along a fishing pole. I said no, and he picked out a rod and reel for me, and some lures. He'd gotten himself a fishing license at the park office and figured I didn't need one, being Native. I told him he was right.

Ryan asked what else I could use. "Nothing I can think of," I said. I helped him find things as he checked off his list. Back at his pickup in the hotel's parking lot, we packed the food into his cooler and metal boxes. We had supper down the street at the Eskimo Inn.

After that we went back to the hotel so Ryan could look over my stuff. As we entered my room, Ryan's eyes went from my duffel bag and small backpack on the bed to the hard plastic rifle case standing in the far corner by the closet. "That doesn't look like a guitar case," he said.

"That's a rifle case. I brought my rifle."

"Hmmm . . . ," he said.

I asked if that was a problem.

"Let's talk about it later," he said, looking away. "We better keep on task while the stores are still open."

We'd been doing so well, but now I wasn't so sure.

Ryan had me spread my stuff all over the bed and around the floor. As he checked out the clothes, he started making a list. There was only one thing I could think about, and that was my rifle. When I came out and asked again if he had a problem with it, he said, "Firearms aren't allowed in Ivvavik National Park. I've got all the info from the park in my room if you want to see it."

"Hey, it's okay," I said with a smile. "I can have a rifle even if you can't. The park was only created with our agreement. The Inuvialuit said it was okay as long as we got to have the exclusive hunting rights. You can ask at the office. That's the way it is, so it's no worries."

"I didn't know that, but I don't doubt it."

That should have settled it about my rifle. Still, Ryan looked unhappy. He wasn't saying why.

"Hey, Ryan," I said with a grin, "you said the fresh food, like the meat, was only for the first week or ten days. I could get us a caribou later on. You should take advantage of me being indigenous."

"I've got canned meat for later."

Trying to keep it light didn't seem to be working. "Are you against hunting?"

"Not at all. I just didn't grow up with it."

"So, what's the problem?"

"The bears."

This made no sense at all. "The bears? The bears are the main reason I brought my rifle. Believe me, we need a rifle for protection."

"I've brought along plenty of protection—pepper spray, bear bangers, and an air horn."

"What are bear bangers?"

"They imitate the sound of a gun."

"A real gun would scare them better."

Again, he hesitated. "Statistically, traveling in grizzly country isn't nearly as dangerous as people think, especially if you take every precaution and know how to behave if you get charged. You're more likely to get hit by lightning than attacked by a bear."

"Not up here. Your chances of getting hit by lightning are about zip."

"I know . . . lightning was unknown in the Arctic, but now it's even starting fires."

"Like where?"

"North slope of Alaska, just last summer. The swath of tundra that burned was twenty miles wide and forty miles long. The frozen ground underneath melted and is releasing huge quantities of methane gas into the atmosphere. As the Arctic warms, you'll see more lightning, and wildfires over here, too."

"Maybe so, but we were talking about bears, and my rifle. What if a grizzly charges you, and all you've got is pepper spray?"

"Pepper spray will disable a bear just fine, without harming it. Nine times out of ten, the experts all agree, it's only a bluff charge. They'll stop ten or fifteen feet short of you. A man with a rifle will shoot before they get that close."

"Of course he would. If it's not a bluff, it would take the bear about half a second to cover those last ten or fifteen feet."

"Everything I've read says the man with the rifle who shoots a charging bear seldom kills it outright. Usually he only wounds it. And a wounded bear is going to retaliate—maul you and maybe kill you. Shooting it actually makes you less safe."

"I wouldn't injure the bear. I'm a really good shot."

"But would you wait until the last second?"

"No way."

"That's what I'm afraid of—killing a bear that was only bluffing."

"Have you ever been charged by a grizzly bear, Ryan?"

"No, but I've been around them in Wyoming and Montana, in Alaska, and last summer in the barren lands east of here."

I didn't say anything. It was irritating to hear him call the tundra "the barren lands." People who aren't from here came up with that. Just because the tundra doesn't have trees on it doesn't mean it's barren. Tundra is a living carpet of hundreds of tiny plants, not barren at all. Barren-ground grizzlies, to my way of thinking, should rightly be called tundra grizzlies.

Ryan broke the silence. "I like our chances without a gun, Nick. Listen to this. For the last twenty-plus years, the Arctic River Company out of Whitehorse has been taking people down the Firth, three trips every summer. They've never had a firearm along—they take the same protection I'm talking about—and they've never had a bear injury. The same goes for the few private parties that raft the Firth every summer. There's never been a mauling on the Firth River."

"There's a first time for everything," I countered. "We never go out on the land—or the ice—without a rifle."

"Hey, Nick, I hear what you're saying and I respect that. My father—our father—felt the same way I do when he kayaked the Northwest Passage. He had a number of encounters with barren-ground grizzlies and one with a polar bear. He didn't take a rifle along for the same reason I don't. If it came down to it, he wasn't willing to kill a bear, and neither am I."

"I still don't get it. Why not?"

"It's their world, not ours. There have to be a few places left where we aren't the top dog."

"I won't use the rifle unless I really have to. That's okay if you can't kill a bear. I'd do it for you."

I could hear the wheels grinding. He scratched his beard and said, "If you killed a bear on my account, I would be responsible."

"The park wouldn't think that if I was the one who killed it."

"I know they wouldn't, but I would."

I hesitated. I'm slow to anger but this was a bit much. "You're saying you don't want me to come unless I don't bring my rifle?"

"I wouldn't put it that way. It means the world to me to have you along. I'm sorry if this sounds crazy to you."

"It's more like, it doesn't make sense."

"We're coming from very different points of view."

"That's for sure," I said, and looked at the floor. I couldn't talk about it anymore. I was so upset, I grabbed my baseball cap, sunglasses, and mosquito repellent, and bolted from the room.

"Nick, I'm sorry, we'll do fine," Ryan called down the hallway. I was already in the lobby and didn't look back.

I wandered through the streets of Inuvik and down to the river, where a barge was unloading. It took me an hour just to settle down, a couple more hours to wrestle with myself over what to do. I didn't want to call home and ask my mother. This was my decision to make. Was it worth the risk?

My mother wouldn't like the idea of me being out on the land for weeks without my rifle. Jonah would say it was pure foolishness.

Still, this was my one chance to have a brother in my life. My mother and grandfather had thought that might be a good thing, and so did I.

There's never been a mauling on the Firth River, I told myself.

I walked up the hill and back to the door of the hotel. It was midnight, with the sun suspended above the north end of the street. Back in my room, I set my alarm. I was going. Unless I went, how was I going to have any stories to tell Jonah about his hunter's paradise?

Morning came brutally early. Ryan hadn't changed his mind. My rifle stayed behind in an old bank vault the hotel used to store valuables.

8

NO WORRIES, JUST KIDDING

Out at the airport, we headed for the hangar of Red Wiley Air Charters. Red greeted us with, "Howdy, boys," and told us to help ourselves to the doughnuts and coffee. The legendary bush pilot was wearing the only outfit I had ever seen him in: beat-up cowboy hat, jumpsuit, and cowboy boots.

Red walked with a limp and spoke with a Texas accent that was still going strong after decades in the North. He was probably the only person in all of northwest Canada that everybody knew on sight. Red had been flying out of Inuvik and into the remote communities for a long, long time. Now and again I would see him at our Northern Store in Aklavik.

Of course he wouldn't know me. I hung back with a doughnut while the two of them made small talk. Pretty quick, the old bush pilot caught my eye and said, "How's Jonah?"

"Hanging on," I said, kind of startled.

"Great hunter, even a better man."

"Thanks. I didn't know you knew him."

"Met him a couple of times. Admired him from afar. People will tell of his deeds for a long, long time."

Ryan backed his pickup into Red's hangar, close to the mountain of gear he had dropped when he drove in from Arizona—the rolled-up raft and all that went with it, no end of canned food, and all the camping stuff. We shuttled everything out to the bush plane, a twin-engine Otter, and unloaded onto the tarmac.

Then we waited. I found myself chewing a fingernail, which isn't like me. I wasn't the only one who was nervous. Ryan kept studying the gear, his forehead bunched up like pressure ridges out on the pack ice. He handed me a butane lighter. I told him I already had a couple. "Keep this one in your pocket," he said.

Finally Red appeared at the door of his office. He put on his sunglasses and limped in our direction. He was famous for having walked away from four crashes.

With a glance at the gear, Red said, "Let's load her up and make history, boys!"

A short while later we were airborne. Up front next to Red, Ryan snapped dozens of pictures as we flew west across the wide delta of the Mackenzie, pausing only to exclaim "Amazing!" and "Awesome!" and suchlike.

This was my first time to see the delta from the air. I spied some of my favorite places to trap muskrats and the exact spot where I got that moose just lately. "Aklavik!" my brother cried, fifteen minutes into the flight. I almost wished I hadn't insisted he take the copilot's seat, after Red had offered it to me.

Our pilot made sure I got a good look at home. I heard the shutter of Ryan's camera whirring. Looking right down on the airstrip and the school and Jonah's house, I nearly lost it. Had I made the right decision?

About ten minutes later we passed over that invisible line between the Northwest Territories and the Yukon Territory. I was keeping my eyes peeled for caribou as we flew surprisingly low over the rolling ups and downs of the treeless tundra, green as green can be.

An hour and a half into the flight, Red finally pulled back on the yoke, and we began to climb. The British Mountains in the heart of Ivvavik National Park lay dead ahead. "Hey, Red," I asked through the intercom, "how come you fly your Otter so close to the ground?"

"Because I'm afraid of heights."

Was he kidding? I really couldn't tell.

Now I was looking down on a jigsaw puzzle of the rugged British Mountains. I didn't like the sound of the name. They should be called the name that they'd gone by for a thousand years and more, before the Europeans made up their own. Jonah would have known our names for the British Mountains and the Firth River. I wished I had asked him.

Below the rounded mountaintops, the steep slopes were clad with a carpet of bright green alpine tundra. The long hours of sunshine the last couple months had melted most of the snow. What remained made white patches on the slopes facing north. I was surprised to see stunted spruce trees growing on the lower flanks of the south-facing slopes. Except for the delta of the Mackenzie, warmed by the river water, the Arctic this far north is too cold for trees. The mountains, I figured, must shield these trees from the winter blasts blowing off the frozen ocean.

Looking nearly straight down out of my window, I spied a herd of big-racked caribou bulls. There were maybe a hundred of them, headed north on their way down a rocky slope. The sight of them had my hunter's heart racing. Mature bulls make their own migration north weeks after the cow caribou head for the calving grounds. The bulls are both lazy and smart. They wait until the snow melts and the traveling gets easier. They catch up with the herd in their own good time.

Minutes short of the Alaska border, we came in sight of a major river valley cutting north through the British Mountains, which seemed to run in rows from east to west. "There's your Firth River, boys," Red Wiley announced.

Red circled around and zeroed in on the upper valley of the Firth River. At the last, it felt like the ground was flying up. We bounced hard on the dry tundra only a couple hundred feet from the river. A couple more bounces on the Otter's balloon tires, and we were down on dry land.

The day was hot, sunny, windless, and muggy—ideal conditions if you're a mosquito. I was barely out of the airplane and they were on me, frantic for a blood meal. I hit the ground wearing my new bug shirt with the hood up and the mosquito netting zipped shut across my neck. My Carhartt jeans were bug-proof as well. All those mozzies could do was whine.

Above me at the side door, Ryan began to hand the gear down. I shuttled the gear well clear of the airplane and returned for the next load fast as I could.

Red got out of the airplane "to see a man about a horse," as he put it. When he got back he told us that this exact spot was where all the Firth River trips launched, and today, June 15, was the traditional opening day. The Arctic River Company out of Whitehorse had always launched the first of their three trips on this date. They weren't running the Firth at all this summer, on account of the bad economy. Only enough people to fill one trip had signed up. The company didn't make any money unless they ran all three.

"There's a chance you'll be seeing a man and his wife from Montana," Red told us. "I'm scheduled to fly them in here nine days from now. Whether they actually show up . . . a lot of times the private parties don't."

It hit me how little I knew about what I was in for. There wasn't going to be a single human being within two hundred miles of us. Being out on the land with Jonah was one thing. Being out on the land with Ryan for three weeks or more was totally a leap of faith.

"I've never had a party stay out near as long as you're talking about," Red said to Ryan.

"Wildlife photography takes nothing but time."

"Sure, but I'm not good with waiting to hear from you. Your sat phone might go on the fritz or get dropped in the river. Give me a date and time of day, weather permitting, for picking you up at Nunaluk Spit."

"Okay, sure," Ryan said. "We'll look for you at ten a.m. on July fifteenth on the Nunaluk Spit."

I fought the urge to climb back into that plane and fly home. A couple minutes later our pilot revved his engines and leaned out his cockpit window to give us a salute. Ryan took pictures as the bush plane rumbled down the tundra on those big balloon tires.

The Otter took off effortlessly, almost jumping into the air. We watched until it disappeared over the mountain. Then we turned to hauling the gear to the shore of the crystal-clear river. I scanned the valley and eyed the mountains all around. Without my rifle, I had never felt so small.

A short walk downstream from where Ryan was pumping up the raft, I came across huge tracks in the mud, unmistakably grizzly. "Hey, Ryan," I called. "Come check this out."

Ryan thought they were the best grizzly tracks he had ever seen. He was all excited about taking pictures, but he read my thought balloon, and said, "We'll keep our bear protection close at hand, in case that big fella is still in the area."

Then and there, he showed me how to use the pepper spray and the bear bangers. Following his lead, I rigged my bear-banger pouch and pepper-spray holster on my belt. They made me feel like I was armed, sort of. Ryan said, "Were the tracks of that grolar bear bigger than these?"

"By a lot."

"You know what? At this moment that grolar bear of yours is the rarest animal on earth. Photos of one in the wild would be the coup of a lifetime."

I didn't say a thing. I didn't want to encourage him. This was crazy talk.

"You know what," Ryan continued. "With the quote in my article to the effect that the grolar bear is probably a product of climate change, I have no doubt that a photo of one would land on the cover of *National Geographic.*"

"Don't even think about it," I said. "You have no idea. That bear would tear you limb from limb."

Big grin. "After I had taken his picture, leaving you to write the article."

I rolled my eyes.

"No worries, just kidding."

We ate a quick lunch; Ryan was anxious to start down the river. He gave me a lightweight pair of rafting gloves and we went to work. When the boat was all rigged, he gave me a safety talk. As he finished that up, I pointed to my life jacket on the ground and asked what the stubby knife in the plastic sheath was all about. It was mounted chest high and upside down. "That's in case you find yourself underwater and tangled in rope," he said. "I've never seen it happen."

I reached for my life jacket. Ryan said, "I don't know about you, but I'm cooking with this bug shirt over my fleece shirt and thermal underwear. I'm stowing my bug shirt. Out on the river, we'll be plenty warm with our life jackets on, and the bugs won't follow us over the freezing-cold water."

I followed suit, then put on my life jacket and snugged the cinches tight. "That's the best life jacket money can buy," Ryan said. "Doesn't matter if you can't swim."

"I can swim pretty good."

"Really? Where did you learn?"

"Indoor pool in Aklavik."

"Really? Aklavik's got a swimming pool?"

"The elders thought it was important. Too many of us used to drown."

Ryan went aboard and took his seat on the big white cooler located back of center in the raft. He put his hands on the oars. "Ready when you are," he called. "Let's go find the caribou."

I untied from the scrub willows, coiled and secured the rope, and shoved the boat into water deep enough for him to begin working the oars. Then I came aboard, keeping low. I settled into position on the cross tube in the front of the raft as the current caught us and we headed downstream.

I looked over my shoulder and found Ryan putting his back to the oars with a smile that radiated deep satisfaction. "So glad to have you with me, little brother," he said.

Greenish like Ryan's eyes, the river ran fast. It was about a hundred feet wide, and I could see every stone on the bottom. The spot where we launched was slipping quickly behind. Downstream, the mountain slopes on the left side descended into the river, here and there covered with dark spruce. Off to the right side the valley floor was open and treeless, the tundra dotted with ponds.

The land was huge and empty-looking, but I knew it was far from empty. The animals were out there. I told my eyes to go into hunting mode. I wanted to be the one who spotted the first wildlife.

It didn't take long. As the raft turned a corner around the flank of the first mountain, I spied something downstream. "Bear!" I yelled. "Bear swimming the river!"

"Where?" big brother yelled back.

"Left side, a couple hundred yards ahead."

Tucking the oar handles under his knees, Ryan leaned forward and unsnapped his big hard-shell camera case. Out came his black digital Nikon. He put it around his neck and started snapping pictures.

Swimming from left to right, the big tundra grizzly was approaching the center of the river. "Maybe it's the one that left the tracks," Ryan panted as he pulled on the oars, aiming to draw close to the bear. He tucked the oars under his knees again and snapped rapid-fire as the grizzly turned its massive head—wide, with frosty tips on the brown fur—and looked right at him.

The river was about to take another bend. The current swept us by the animal. Ryan snapped more pictures as the bear reached shallow water and rose from the river, water streaming from its sides.

Hurriedly, Ryan put his camera away and cinched the straps tight that secured the camera case. As we rounded the bend, he began to spin the boat so he could see downstream.

As the front of the boat swung around I saw what lay ahead of us a split second before my brother did. My heart was in my throat. Shore to shore, the river was blocked by ice. It was three feet high, and we were headed straight for it.

Ryan pivoted the boat and rowed toward the right shore with all his strength. There wasn't nearly enough time. "Nick!" I heard my brother cry as the raft was swept sideways against the white wall of ice. The heavily loaded raft flipped over and sent us flying headlong into the freezing river.

9

DISASTER

The shock of getting thrown into the river and under the ice took my breath away—what little I had in my lungs as we capsized. The cold felt like a lethal jolt of electricity. All was confusion and chaos. Flailing, I righted myself in the swift-running current and knocked my head against a ceiling of solid ice. Underwater I found no air, no gap between the river and the ice.

From the corner of my eye I saw Ryan in the same deadly fix. The water was cold beyond belief. I panicked. This was it. There was no escape.

I didn't know how long I could hold out. Not much

longer. After that one glimpse I had lost sight of my brother.

As I got swept along, my head kept bumping the ice, and still I couldn't find an air pocket. The end was coming quick. I was going to black out. It wasn't like they say, with your whole life flashing before your eyes, people's faces and all that, not even Jonah's. Disbelief and fear, that's all there was.

Ahead and to the right, I saw something different from the ceiling of ice all lit by sunlight: a dark patch, almost black. What was that?

Somehow I connected to Jonah, a memory of him telling me what to do. I had to swim toward that dark circle. Stroking and kicking hard as I could, I remembered why. The darkness meant open water.

The river was running so fast, I would have only one chance. Against the force of the current, how was I going to pull myself onto the ice?

Knife, I thought. Eyes locked on that nearing dark patch, I pulled the rescue knife from my life jacket as I kept stroking with my free arm. Kicking hard with both legs, I got there. Bursting through the dark water and into the open air, I stabbed the stubby knife into the ice all the way to the hilt.

The knife held. I kicked hard and dragged myself out of the river and onto the ice.

I lay there gasping and heaving for breath, frozen to the bone. I was shuddering and shaking so bad, I didn't think I could stand up. Then I realized I shouldn't even try. The ice might break underneath me. I crawled on my elbows toward the shore.

At the shoreline I clawed my way onto the rocks. Ryan was nowhere to be seen. I stumbled along the grassy top of the riverbank. Fifty yards farther on, where the ice jam ended, the river rushed downstream, open and clear. I spied the raft way down there, bottom side up. A couple of seconds, and it passed out of view around the bend.

Where was my brother? I scanned the shore beyond the ice, both sides of the river—no sign of him. "Ry-an!" I called, shivering and shaking. "Ryyyyy-an!"

In a full-on panic I broke into a run, or tried to. I tripped over my own feet, then got up and kept going. Ground squirrels standing by their burrows dived for cover. Where the ice ended, I made my way down to the river's edge. Scrambling along the rocky shore, I fell two, three times. I had next to no control over my shuddering limbs. Where was Ryan? Had he drowned, was he dead? Was I alone?

I staggered down the shore, falling and rising and shaking and falling. All the winters I had been through, even those times I had been on the windy sea ice at thirty below, I had never experienced cold like this. I had to warm up, and soon. My body core had gotten much too cold. "Ryyy-an!" I screamed.

Don't give up, you have to find him. Maybe he blacked out and he's still in the water. If so, you have to pull him out fast. I scanned and scanned and saw nothing.

From the corner of my eye I caught some movement downstream, on the far side of the river. Then nothing. I ran past a long clump of brush for a better look, and glimpsed a flash of orange, an orange life jacket. It was Ryan, out of the water and stumbling along the rocky shore. Just then he tripped and fell.

"Ryan!" I yelled at the top of my lungs. He couldn't hear me over the sound of the river. "Ry—an! Ry—an!" I yelled, then stumbled downriver until we were opposite each other. By this time he had seen me. "Nick!" he screamed. "Nick, you're alive!"

My brother had been in the water longer than me, and had even less control over his body. He fell down, got up, fell down again.

I was thinking clearly enough to have this much figured out: I wasn't capable of swimming to his side and he wasn't capable of swimming to mine.

Ryan got to his knees. I cupped my hands to my mouth and hollered loud as I could: "SHOULD . . . I . . . TRY . . . TO . . . CROSS . . . ON . . . THE . . . ICE?"

Ryan managed to regain his feet. "DON'T TRY! IT MIGHT BREAK! STAY THERE, MAKE FIRE!"

My hand went to my trousers pocket. The lighter he'd given me was still there. There wasn't a bit of driftwood on the shore. I looked around for the nearest trees.

On Ryan's side of the Firth, spruce trees grew on the mountain slope that rose out of the river. My side was valley floor, open tundra, most of it grassy and dry. The low places held ponds and muskeg swamp. My eyes landed on a clump of spruce trees on a knoll a couple hundred feet downstream and a couple hundred feet back from the river. "OKAY," I yelled.

I turned and began to climb the riverbank as best I could manage. "SORRY!" Ryan called after me.

Atop the bank, I steered for those trees. *No time to lose*, I kept telling myself.

The clouds had thickened since Red had taken off, and the temperature had dropped. How much I couldn't tell. The wind was beginning to rise. I wasn't shivering and shaking anymore, and that wasn't good. It was like I had turned to stone.

Pursued by the bugs, I climbed the knoll to the clump of spruce trees. An opening that faced the river led to a small clearing in the miniature grove.

First thing I did was to force my clawlike fingers into my pocket. Pulling the lighter out was anything but easy. It fell to the ground, small and red. I set it on a rock where the air might dry it out.

No taller than twenty feet, the trees huddled close to one another, their outer branches extending all the way to the ground. The inner branches were long dead from lack of sunlight. I crawled in on my hands and knees and went after the dead stuff. I was wearing those rafting gloves Ryan had given me. They helped as I broke off handfuls of brittle, dead branch tips skinny as soda straws.

By the time I collected some thicker wood, I could barely function. I propped my kindling against a rock, like Jonah had showed me when I wasn't any taller than his waist. I knelt down and tried to make my thumb turn that little metal wheel on the lighter.

For the life of me, I couldn't do it. Couldn't get my thumb on it, couldn't work the thumb when I did. Mosquitoes were buzzing in my ears and landing on my face, drawing blood, no doubt, but I couldn't feel them.

For crying out loud. I was beyond desperate, and that wasn't helping. After a few more attempts I thought to take a glove off, and warmed my hand in my armpit. After a minute I was able to work my thumb and fingers. I tried the lighter again. The flame sputtered out the first couple times, but then it held.

The kindling caught, and the flames grew quickly. I added the bigger stuff and went for more. Satisfied that my fire wouldn't die out, I stripped, wrung out my clothes, and spread them out on the branches. As long as I stood in the smoke, I was out of reach of the mosquitoes.

As I stoked the fire and warmed myself through and through, a front was on its way in. The clouds were thickening and the wind started blowing hard enough to make the mosquitoes go to ground.

By now I was coming out of the immediate shock, enough to get a grasp on the situation—complete disaster. I remembered Ryan saying that even if we flipped, which wasn't going to happen, all we would lose was our sunglasses.

What about my baseball cap, Ryan? What about the bear spray off my hip? That big tundra grizzly we saw in the river might appear at any second. How are you going to get your boat back? You fool, you clueless fool!

"SORRY," he had hollered.

What a mistake this had been from the very beginning, the whole thing, and me getting sucked into it on account of him being my brother. Finding huge numbers of caribou to photograph—what were the chances? I'd lived up here my whole life and never seen thousands. Never even saw five hundred. And the article he was going to write. What did he know about caribou? How could he write about us, when he wasn't even a hunter? "Sorry, Nick, you can't bring your rifle."

No more than two miles down the river, we'd lost everything. Everything! What was his plan for getting the boat back? The satellite phone was on the raft, and the raft was on its way to the Beaufort Sea. What were our chances of getting rescued without the sat phone—approximately zero?

Nice, Ryan, really nice.

Even our bug shirts were on the boat. He'd said we wouldn't need them when we were out on the river, over the freezing water. I'd stowed my mosquito repellent too—afraid of losing it out of my pocket!

Over the next couple hours I dried my clothes by the fire, careful not to scorch them. At last they were dry, and I put them back on, along with my boots, which were still wet but not sopping. *Never try to dry them by the fire*, Jonah had told me a long time ago. *They'll get ruined for sure.*

Thoughts of Jonah helped me push back the anger and the fear. I was up against it, but not nearly as bad as him. He'd be expecting me to live through this no matter how bad it got. I had to get ahold of myself and think positive. Who knows, maybe the raft had gotten hung up on something downstream. Maybe Ryan was already down there doing something about it.

It was time I checked to see if my brother was even alive. As I left the sheltering trees, I had little doubt that rain was on the way. Unfortunately, our rain gear was on the raft. I still had my waterproof watch—that was something. The time was 8:35 p.m.

Smoke was rising from back in the trees a ways down the far side of the Firth. I got ready to holler Ryan out to the shore. No need—he was standing at river's edge farther downstream with his eyes on my side of the river. No more than a hundred yards from where I stood, thirty or so caribou bulls were making their way down to the river to drink. Only the width of the Firth separated Ryan from those magnificent animals with their huge racks. It must be killing him not to be able to take their pictures.

I didn't feel sorry for him. If he hadn't been so busy taking pictures, he would have seen the ice sooner. There would have been time to row to shore.

From our separate sides of the river, we watched the bulls go. Ryan walked upriver until he was straight across from me, and hollered that he had seen smoke from my fire. "YOU OKAY?"

"I'M OKAY!"

"THANK GOD!" He yelled that he thought it was going to rain. "STAY DRY, NICK. STAY PUT."

77

Duh, I thought. I fought the urge to go sarcastic on him. That wouldn't help a thing. "GOT IT," I yelled back. "WHAT NOW?"

"I'M GOING TO TRY TO FIND THE RAFT. YOU STAY WHERE YOU ARE. MAYBE IT DIDN'T GO FAR."

"WHEN ARE YOU COMING BACK?"

"TOMORROW AT THE LATEST! IF I DON'T FIND IT, I'LL SWIM ACROSS TOMORROW. WE WILL GO FARTHER, LOOK FOR IT TOGETHER."

"GOT IT!"

Suddenly there came a huge cracking sound, then a second crack. I'd heard that sound my whole life—ice breaking up.

We both looked upriver, seeing nothing at first. Half a minute later, around a bend, here came the ice, hundreds and thousands of chunks of it, some small, some as big as refrigerators and pickup trucks. The shore-to-shore ice jam that had flipped our raft was soon passing us by in bits and pieces, grinding and scraping and hissing and jostling as it headed for the sea.

Ten minutes later the river was running clear. Every last trace of the ice had gone out. No doubt we were both thinking the same thing. Too bad we didn't camp where Red let us off, and launch the next day.

"I BETTER GET GOING!" Ryan hollered.

"GOTTA CHASE THE RAFT!" He waved and started hiking downriver at a brisk pace.

It crossed my mind I might never see him again. The Arctic has a way of swallowing people up. You make a big mistake, most likely you pay for it.

"GOOD LUCK!" I shouted after him. Angry and annoyed and irritated as I was, I was depending on him to come through.

10

MY SIDE OF THE RIVER

Watchful for that grizzly we had seen swimming the river, I climbed over the top of the riverbank. My fear was rising. I shouldn't have let Ryan split us up.

The wind was buffeting my little spruce grove on the knoll. Dark clouds were spitting rain as I came to the clearing among the trees. The fire was out, and I had used up all the dead wood within reach. I crawled into the trees and found a spot to wait out the weather under the dense, sheltering branches.

Sitting there with zero bear protection, my back against a spruce trunk, I was spooked nearly to puking. Barren-ground grizzlies—tundra grizzlies, Arctic grizzlies, whatever you want to call them—are more aggressive than grizzlies below the Arctic Circle. They have a shorter food-gathering season, which means they have to eat mostly meat. And to get enough meat—mainly caribou, dead or alive—they have to fight each other for it. Only the fierce survive.

The rain broke loose just before midnight. The layers of live spruce branches above me did a good enough job as a roof. My life jacket shed the drips that found their way through, and the grove knocked the wind down. Lacking rain gear, I was thankful for my thermal underwear, my tight-weave trousers, and my long-sleeved, long-tailed shirt of synthetic fleece.

I kept thinking about Ryan, wondering how he was doing. Was he taking shelter or still searching for the raft? He'd better watch his step. Break a leg, and we would be even worse off. What about his pepper spray and bear bangers? I couldn't remember seeing them on his hip. Had he lost them under the ice?

I slept in fits. Morning came dark and dreary. During a break in the weather I went to the river. It was running huge, nothing like the river we had started on. I wasn't surprised. Our ground can't absorb much rain. A few feet below the surface it's permafrost, frozen year-round.

Ryan had talked about swimming across to my side, but that wouldn't be possible anytime soon. The rain was moving in again. I hustled back to the trees.

Twelve hours after it had started, the deluge stopped for good. The sun came out, and so did the mosquitoes. I went to the river and caked my face and neck with mud.

To my surprise, Ryan emerged from the trees on the other side. He looked awful, all scratched up. As for bear protection, he didn't have any. Both of us had lost our pepper spray off our belts when we went under the ice. He'd also been stripped of his bear banger pouch. Mine was packed away on the boat.

"DIDN'T FIND THE RAFT," my brother roared over the raging river.

"WHAT IF IT GOES ALL THE WAY TO THE OCEAN?" I hollered.

"IT'LL GET CAUGHT ON A ROCK! LET'S GO FIND IT! TRY TO STAY IN SIGHT OF EACH OTHER!"

"GOT IT!" I yelled back. He was right, there was nothing to be gained from staying put—everything we needed was on the raft. But what were our chances of catching up with it?

The mosquitoes were bad. Ryan took his bug juice out of his pocket and dabbed some on. I took my gloves off and knelt to rub more mud on my face, neck, and scalp.

We started walking. On my side of the river—the eastern side, the right-hand side as we headed north to the sea—the going was fairly easy for the time being.

The terrain was much rougher on Ryan's side, with steep slopes crowding the shore. With no trails it was slow going, especially for him.

The mosquitoes were getting to my eyelids, where I had no mud. Their high-pitched whine was making me crazy. In Aklavik we spend most of June indoors. Then we head for the windy coast, as much to get away from bugs as for the fishing and whaling.

Here and now, the coast was eighty miles away.

Come midnight, the low-hanging sun was blocked by a mountain but gave plenty of daylight. When it rose over a ridge around 2:00 a.m. we were still trudging downriver. The Firth wasn't brimful like before but was running way too high and fast for Ryan to swim across.

Less than forty-eight hours since we'd eaten, I already felt like I was starving. I thought of my ancestors—their legendary endurance during times of starvation—but couldn't convince my stomach to stop whining. I thought about throwing rocks at the ground squirrels standing sentry at their burrows. *Sik-sik*, we call them, after the sound they make. From experience I knew that my chances of nailing one were worse than poor.

I came upon the site of a bear dig where a grizzly had bulldozed the ground-hugging tundra vegetation with its enormous claws and massive forelimbs. The excavation was eight feet across and a couple deep. That grizzly was a picky eater. The bear had left behind the heads of five ground squirrels, eyes open with terror. The sight made me lose my appetite for *sik-sik*.

Some places I came to, the valley floor was riddled with clumps of tussock grass. Afraid I'd break an ankle, I picked my way carefully among the hummocks. As much as possible, I walked the riverbank so my brother and I could keep an eye on each other. Whenever I lost track of him, I stayed put. Soon as he located me, it was time to start walking again.

Around 8:00 a.m. I came to a side stream with a pool deep as my chest. It was holding a few char, five-pounders or so. Too bad I had no way to fish them out.

I needed to find a shallow place to wade this creek. I turned upstream and immediately ran into grizzly tracks in a mud patch among the man-high willows. My hackles went up and I backed away from the bushes, keeping to the tundra. Across the river, Ryan had caught sight of my detour and was waiting for me to ford the creek.

Twenty yards upstream, the creek ran in two channels around a gravel island. The narrow channel on my side of the island was the shallower of the two. I was about to start wading when I spotted a big char holding in shin-deep water under the bank. At the head of the channel, the water ran only ankle deep. I got an idea.

With a rush, I jumped into the channel just below

the fish. The char darted upstream and I gave chase. Where the water got too shallow, the big fish turned and darted back in my direction. It was going to run past me or between my legs unless I did something fast. I threw my body down, flat out across the channel. The fish headed back upstream.

I got up and ran after it. This time the char tried to force its way through the ankle-deep water at the head of the channel. I leaped on it and pinned it with my forearm, then bashed its head with a rock.

I held up that silvery char for my brother to see. Ryan got all excited and yelled, "BRAVO, LITTLE BROTHER!" from across the river. I kind of liked him calling me that.

I took out my hunting knife and cut a filet from either side of the backbone. The red flesh was absolutely delicious. It was a shame big brother missed out.

We kept going. I felt stronger even though I was still bleary from exhaustion. By noon the upper valley of the Firth was pinching to a close with mountain slopes crowding both sides of the river.

After a bit we reached a spot where it got rougher yet. On Ryan's side, a cliff rose hundreds of feet out of the river. Ryan yelled that he was going to have to climb above and around. It was up to me to search this stretch of the river for the raft. I should wait for him at the first place where it looked like he could get back to the river.

I watched Ryan climb up the edge of a rockslide until he disappeared in the trees up above the cliff. Queasy with him gone again, I headed downriver, keeping my eye out for the raft. The terrain on my side of the Firth was getting rough, and I had to struggle to get a visual on every stretch of water. The stakes were life-and-death. There was food on the boat, not to mention the satellite phone and bear protection.

It was maddening to try to figure out where Ryan could get back to the river. It continued to be way rough and steep on his side. I kept going on mine. At two in the afternoon the sun was blazing. I was overheating but didn't shed my life jacket, tempted as I was to carry it in my hand. It would help protect my vitals if I got mauled by a bear.

I was falling-down weary but kept putting one foot in front of the other. My throat was so dry I could barely muster saliva. I realized I was getting dehydrated, which was stupid with water so close at hand. I worked my way down to the river, looking upstream and down for the easiest place to drink. Upstream the bank was choked with chest-high willows. Downstream the willows thinned out.

I turned downstream toward an open spot on the shore where a rock slab angled gently into the water—a perfect place to get a drink and even to lie down and get a little rest.

As I approached the slab, I caught the scent of decay. That wasn't good. I froze in my tracks and looked down the shore. Not thirty feet away, a massive, humped bear was lying asleep beside the bloody, half-eaten carcass of a bull caribou.

In a heartbeat, I knew I was in a deadly predicament. Without taking a breath, I looked over my left shoulder to make certain of my escape route.

Before I made my move, I looked back at the bear.

Too late. The grizzly was awake and staring right at me. The bear erupted in a full-throated roar. In an instant, it was on its feet, charging me with terrifying speed.

You don't run from a charging grizzly, but this was no bluff charge. This bear was protecting a carcass and out of its mind with rage. I took one, two steps. Another instant and the bear would be on me. I had only one chance, one way of escape. I leaped into the river.

11

A GAUNTLET OF GRIZZLIES

Once more I found myself in the ice-cold river. The shock hit me like ten thousand volts. Floating on my back, I swept with my arms to get away from the shore. Over my shoulder I saw the bear rushing into the river after me. I got on my belly and swam hard, arm over arm.

When I reached the main current, and was taken by its power and speed, I flipped onto my back again with my legs pointed downstream. The bear had given up the chase. It was already climbing ashore next to the carcass.

I knew I should try to haul out on the opposite shore, but the river was too swift along the west bank, the shoreline too rugged.

I let myself get swept farther away from that bear.

Ahead, the river was dividing into two channels around an island of gravel. The tip of that island might be my last chance to escape the cold that was squeezing the life out of me.

The current was fast, and the island was nearing. I let the life jacket buoy me along, saving what strength the cold hadn't already sapped. Halfway to the head of the island I saw antlers and carcasses in the shallows there—two more bull caribou. There were ravens on them, but no bears as far as I could tell.

I couldn't afford to miss my chance at the island. I swam with everything I had left to break out of the current. I managed to escape it—just barely—and struggled into the shallows on my hands and knees. The dead caribou, I noticed dully, were bloated. Then I smelled them. The ravens took a few hops and flew away.

Try as I might, I couldn't muster the strength to stand up. I crawled out of the shallows and onto the dry gravel, heaving for breath. When I sat up, motion on the eastern shore caught my eye: a grizzly feeding on a bull caribou. I was all confused. Was this the same grizzly that charged me before?

No, the answer came finally. Same side of the river, different caribou, different grizzly.

Suddenly the bear became aware of me and stood up tall to get a better look. Its ears went erect. The big brown bear huffed at me two, three times, then swayed back and forth and clacked its jaws. I stayed down in hopes I wouldn't appear as a threat.

With a ferocious growl, the grizzly went back onto all fours. It was no more than a hundred feet away, and could swim the channel between us in no time. Froze up as I was, I should have been running up and down that island, trying to get my circulation going, but that would provoke a charge. I should have been taking off my clothes and wringing them out. I couldn't chance that either.

The bear went back to rending flesh and feeding on its prize. Like a dog over a bone, it paused frequently to growl at me.

The big brownie didn't seem aware that another grizzly was coming down the bank to the river. This one was big too, and battle-scarred around the shoulders. The new bear stopped to survey the situation and smell the air, then lumbered on down.

Soon as the intruder reached the riverside, the bear on the carcass rushed it. The two rose and came at each other, roaring horribly. They met standing upright in a fury of claws and teeth.

The battle raged on, up and down the shore. Both were eight feet tall and massive, but the newcomer was more aggressive and able to draw more blood. The grizzly that had been there first finally backed away from the carcass.

After skulking for a few minutes, and feinting as if it was going to rejoin the battle, the defeated bear turned its attention to the island and the two carcasses right next to me. It waded into the river and began to swim, heading my way.

I lurched to my feet. As the grizzly came ashore, I was wading into the far channel. I plunged headfirst into deep water and let the river take me again. The current swept me past the foot of the island and into the powerful water where the channels around the island became one again. I was in a panic to get out of the river but didn't see a place where I could. Down a long straightaway, I floated past eight more grizzlies on carcasses—both sides of the river—including a mother grizzly and two small cubs.

The racing river swept me around another bend. Dozens more drowned caribou appeared, all bulls, none with bears on them. Their eyes were missing, pecked out by the birds.

A gravel bar appeared ahead, on the left side, my last chance. As poorly as my limbs were responding, I didn't think I could get there, but I had to try. The fast water alongside the gravel bar swept me halfway down its length in a frightening hurry. I swam with one last effort, out of the current and into the slowing water at the foot of the gravel bar. In knee-deep water I struggled to stand, stumbled onto dry land, and collapsed.

I was content to lie there. I wasn't shaking, and the cold wasn't painful anymore.

Something was bothering my rest. *Never say die*, I heard a voice saying. The voice was my own. Then I knew. If I didn't get up now, I never would.

I tried to rise and fell down. I tried again, staggered to my feet, and lurched into motion. I had to keep moving or I had no chance. Up and down the gravel bar I stumbled, falling down and getting up and throwing my arms back and forth, stamping my feet, slapping my sides and my legs with my frozen hands. I had to keep my heart pumping.

It would be warmer, I thought, if I could get away from the ice-cold river at least a little. I crawled up the riverbank and onto a carpet of tundra. I had been in the water longer than the first time when I was under the ice. I couldn't have started a fire even if I had trees within reach, which I didn't. With my frozen fingers, stiff as claws, it was all I could manage to get my life jacket and sopping-wet clothes off.

I was in for a bloodletting. There was only a breath of wind, not enough to keep the mosquitoes down. I hurled myself into a frenzy, jogging in place and slapping the circulation back into my limbs as I swatted mosquitoes. I couldn't take this anymore.

I stifled the urge to scream. The sound of my voice, full of fear, might bring the bears.

Soon as I'd wrung as much water as I could from my clothes, I put those long sleeves and trousers back on. The mosquitoes came at my face. Lying down on a slab of rock facing the sun with my life jacket under my head and draped over my face, I gave up. I'd done what I could do. I was going to recover or not.

Like a ground squirrel coming out of stone-cold hibernation, I came gradually back to life. It was the heat of that scorching midsummer day that revived me. All done in, bears or no bears, I fell asleep on that slab of rock.

It must have been the cooling air that woke me. My clothes were dry. I was in the shade and the daylight had dimmed. My watch said 11:00 p.m.

I sat up feeling exposed, all out in the open like I was. I looked to my right and saw nothing. To my left, no more than thirty feet away, an enormous white wolf was rising to its feet. The wolf had been lying there watching me for who knows how long. Now it was sizing me up.

My hand went to my hip. On second thought I didn't draw my hunting knife. I might provoke the animal. There was nothing threatening about the wolf's body language. Behind those staring yellow eyes, its intelligence was obvious.

Many a time Jonah had seen lone wolves take down healthy, adult caribou, even bulls. Our Arctic wolves are that big and powerful. These days, we don't see them very often. When we're out on our snowmobile in search of spring bears, we might spot a wolf. I killed one once when I was with Jonah. It ran like the wind soon as it heard us. Neither of us felt proud about running it down, but we didn't pass up the chance. Their fur makes great ruffs for winter parkas, second-best only to wolverine.

To be this close to this white wolf—standing so tall on its legs, with the wind rustling its fur, its curious eyes still taking me in—kind of shook me to the core. This was the most magnificent animal I had seen in my life. I remembered Jonah saying that nobody knows why they don't hunt us when they could, like bears do once in a while, especially polar bears. Wolves won't kill you for the meat on your bones, but they'll help themselves if they come across your dead body. Why is that?

I trusted that the wolf meant me no harm, and it turned out I was right. I even spoke to the animal, and it perked up its ears and listened. I told the wolf how hungry I was, and how grateful I would be if it would bring me something to eat, only please don't swallow it first—I wasn't partial to throw-up. I really did say all of that and more. I was half out of my mind. It kept me calm, and the wolf seemed to find it of interest.

The wolf decided it had seen enough of me. It turned and trotted off. When it turned and looked at me again, I called, "Thanks for not ripping my throat out." The wolf trotted away, this time without looking back.

On the spot I decided I would never shoot another wolf.

12

YOU HAVE TO BE PATIENT

In the wake of the wolf, I went to the edge of that shelf of tundra above the river and took a look down. The river was back down to what it had been before the big rainstorm. The deluge that drowned all those caribou had flushed on through. They should have waited before trying to cross. Like Jonah always said, they're great swimmers but don't always make good choices.

And now I found myself on Ryan's side of the river, the western side. I tilted my head back and scanned the slopes above, treeless here. He wasn't up there. Ryan had said to look for him at the first obvious place for him to get down. This wasn't it—far too steep and rugged. I had to go farther downstream to find the place where he would come back to the river.

I got going, with no choice but to cross slopes that fell steeply into the river. Sometimes I had to crab-walk across tongues of loose, sliding rock in order to continue. One thing was for sure: I wasn't going to swim the river to get back to easier walking on the other side.

Midmorning the next day, the mountains finally pulled back from the river. I walked the falling spine of a ridge onto flat ground, a bright green tundra bench that sat just above the river. There was one just like it across the river from me. Here was that "first obvious place" for us to get back together.

There I waited, out in the open with my bright orange life jacket draped on top of a lone, spindly spruce. Maybe Ryan had already swum the river, like he said he was going to, to get back to "my side." If so, he would easily spot the life jacket and me over here.

As the sun made its big circle around the sky, I gathered firewood, made a fire, and laid on lots of green branches. Might as well make sure he doesn't miss me, I figured. My smoke signals didn't reel him in. I thought of moving on but decided that would be a huge mistake. Without a doubt, this was the first obvious place.

You have to be patient, I could hear Jonah saying, and I remembered the time we went out on the sea ice together to hunt seals the way the ancestors had, and his father still did when Jonah was young. I was only nine, still a hyper kid, but I loved hunting. Jonah had been taking me out with him since I was five.

We didn't have a dog team like my great-grandfather did to get us out onto the Beaufort Sea—we went on Jonah's snowmobile—but we did make an igloo three nights in a row. Instead of netting the seals under the ice or stalking them with a rifle from behind a white blind like we do these days, Jonah was going to try to take one at close range like it used to be done.

When we finally found a breathing hole—small and glazed over, as difficult to locate as a needle in a haystack—Jonah brought a small feather out from under his parka. He stuck it into the side of the breathing hole, then took his position. He crouched with his father's harpoon in hand, and he waited. And waited. I mean, for hours.

When the time finally came, and that feather vibrated slightly to signal the rising seal, Jonah had to be ready to strike in a split second, and he was. He struck with force and accuracy. I've always enjoyed seal meat, but that seal was the best ever.

In the times before our ancestors even had dogs, Jonah told me, and they pulled their heavy sleds under their own power, there were winters when the seals were hard to come by, and the people would starve. Sometimes they went weeks without food. They had to wait. They had to be patient.

Right now, I had to be patient and wait for my brother. If there'd been a mix-up, I was only going to make it worse by running around on the tundra looking for him.

Exhaustion pulled me down. I slept the rest of the day. Around ninety minutes after midnight I woke to the sun rising over a ridge, got my fire going again, made more smoke. I went to counting how many days it had been. I pieced it all together by how many midnights had gone by. The accident happened on Day 1. This was the beginning of Day 5. I took out my hunting knife and made five notches on its leather sheath.

I went back to sleep. By midmorning I had been waiting at "the first obvious place" for twenty-four hours. My stomach hurt from worry and hunger. I had remembered to keep drinking water but was getting weak and light-headed.

As for my brother, I was fearing the worst. He got mauled by a bear, he broke a leg, he fell off a cliff. He drowned. The mountains had swallowed him up.

Did it still make sense to stay put? No, it didn't: too much time had passed. I decided to give him until noon.

Noon arrived. If I stayed, I was going to get weaker

and weaker until I wouldn't be strong enough to walk out. The coast was probably still forty or fifty miles away. Once I reached the coast, I had a chance of being spotted. Now and again, motorboats out of Shingle Point came this far west.

Once I got there, it wouldn't be a good idea to sit and wait for a boat that might happen by. Chances would be poor, before I starved out. Better to keep walking. From the mouth of the Firth, if I headed east a few miles, I would be looking at Herschel Island. The island sat only a couple of miles offshore; I'd been there once with Jonah. The whole coast of the Yukon Territory was littered with driftwood . . . I could start a signal fire visible from the island's historical park at the old whaling station.

Better get going, I told myself. I started downriver, keeping an eye out for the raft but with no real hope of coming across it.

Same time the next day, I put a sixth notch on my knife sheath. I hadn't eaten a thing since that one char I caught. I was making a poor showing as an aboriginal hunter.

Just ahead, the river ran fast and white as it dropped between walls of stone rising along the shore. I remembered Ryan saying that after the "mountain reach" of the Firth, the "canyon reach" began at Mile 40. That was where we would run the first major rapid, about halfway to the ocean.

At least I knew where I was, for what good it would do me.

Broad shelves of stone flanked the entrance of the canyon. I climbed the shelves on my side to their high point. Thirty feet below me, the Firth cascaded with a roar over slabs of rock heaving out of the river like whales.

I looked downriver to the tail end of the rapid and beyond. A speck of color and a bit of movement on the other side of the river caught my eye—something bright orange atop the shallow canyon. I squinted and made out a man wearing a life jacket, walking north toward the ocean. My heart leaped.

It was amazing what seeing Ryan did for my legs. Strength surged back into them, and I broke into a trot on the tundra. What was he doing on what had been "my side" of the river? Hadn't he planned to wait for me on this side? He said he was going to swim over to the east side, but wasn't that after we met up again?

I gradually closed the gap, but by the time I drew even with him across the river, he was angling away from the canyon rim. Ryan was moving slow, and he stumbled. I hollered and hollered, but over the sound of the river he didn't hear me. He disappeared behind a huge mound of rock that rose above the river.

I couldn't lose him again. One of us was going to have to swim the river—and it might as well be me.

There were breaks here and there in the walls of the shallow canyon. Not very far ahead, a slot between the cliffs would make it easy for me to get down to the water. Directly across, fifty-foot high cliffs rose from the river, but those cliffs ended in fewer than a hundred yards. The riverbank was grassy there, easy to climb out on.

What about the river—was it swimmable? Its deep, dark green water was more roily than I would have liked, stirred up from falling through the rapid, but the Firth wasn't very wide here, less than a hundred feet across. The day was warm and sunny. If I swam arm over arm, I wouldn't be in the water very long.

This is crazy, I told myself. Not really, I answered back, not if you swim it fast enough. It's the amount of time you're in the water that makes it deadly. It's not that far across, and the river is running as low as it's going to get. The day is hot and sunny.

Fish or cut bait, I told myself. After studying the water one more time, I tightened the cinches of my life jacket and dove in.

13

SWAPPING STORIES

Expecting the shock of the freezing water and the numbness that followed within seconds, I wasn't as frightened this time. Crossing the seam between the slower water and the fast, I swam hard to maintain a forty-five-degree angle to the current.

It turned into more of a battle than I thought I was in for. A boil of water got hold of me and I lost my angle. I found myself headed directly downstream.

Now I was frightened. No turning back, I told myself. I got my bearings, got my angle back again, and swam harder than before, across the major current and across the seam into the slower water along the eastern shore.

I could still work my fingers when I got out at the foot

of the grassy slope. I'd only been in the water a couple of minutes and I wasn't hypothermic, not that I wasn't feeling the chill. My heart was hammering as I climbed that grassy slope, sucking wind as I came over the top.

No more than fifty feet away, my brother was about to pass by. I barely had the breath left to call his name. "Ryan," I panted.

His head jerked in my direction. At first my brother was startled, like he was seeing a ghost. The emotions flooding his face, in his eyes, defy description. Disbelief and joy were battling it out, and joy was winning.

Then he broke up, really lost it. Broke down and cried. The grief he'd been feeling, I guess, was finding its way out.

We met in a bear hug, bumping our bulky life jackets, me dripping wet. He looked haggard as could be. I'm sure I didn't look so good myself—sunburned, bug-bitten, half-starved.

Ryan's sunburn was worse than mine, but his lips were okay and he didn't have very many bites. "Why are you all wet, little brother?"

"I was on the other side of the river—just swam across. Man, it's good to see you! I was worried out of my skull!"

"Same here! What a mix-up! I swam to your side much sooner than I expected I'd be able to, and you swam to my side. All this time I've been looking for you on this side. I was afraid you'd been mauled by a bear, killed by a bear!"

I was so pumped up with adrenaline and so relieved, I felt giddy. "Did you see a bear?" I asked with a straight face, like Jonah would do.

"See a bear . . . there's a stretch back there that's lousy with bears—huge grizzlies!"

"Lousy with bears? You sure?"

"You didn't see them?"

I broke out in a smile. "Just kidding. I saw lots of bears, and the dead caribou they were gorging on."

"Why'd you cross over?"

"It wasn't on purpose. I made the mistake of surprising a grizzly on a carcass, real close-up. When he charged, it wasn't a bluff. The river was my only chance to get away."

"Good grief. And I told you there's never been a mauling on the Firth River. You would've been the first."

"For sure. How 'bout you, Ryan? Did you get charged?"

"Twice, from about a hundred feet. Both times the grizzly pulled up right in front of me. Stood up, roared at me, then hustled back to the carcass it had staked out."

"Was it scary, big brother?"

"Scary? On the one-to-ten pucker scale, it was a

nineteen. Even if I had my pepper spray, it would've been a nineteen. But you don't sound like you were scared."

"I wasn't scared. Terrified, was more like it. I counted eleven bears. How about you?"

"Fourteen! Thank God we're both alive and intact!"

I couldn't resist. "If you'd had my rifle, would you have used it?"

"No, but the whole time I was wishing I had let you bring it—for your own protection."

"That's okay. I wouldn't have fired it anyway."

"Really?"

"It would have been on the raft."

"Hmmm, you're right about that."

Ryan had me tell the rest of my story, then he told me more of his. Shortly after swimming to "my side" of the river, he heard the awful sound of bears in combat. When he worked his way close enough to get a look, he saw a mother grizzly battling to protect her cubs from a big male. The boar had already driven her off a carcass, and now he was after her cubs. She gave more than she got, and was able to escape with both cubs.

After seeing those first four bears, Ryan took a detour away from the river. He was afraid to stick close to the river, where he might run into more grizzlies on more drowned caribou. When he returned to the river a couple of hours downstream, he searched half a day without even finding a footprint. "By then," Ryan said, "I'd gotten to thinking you were back upstream in that lousy-with-bears stretch, and had gotten mauled or killed or worse."

"Worse?" I asked with a grin.

"Eaten, maybe?"

"I guess that would be worse. Then what did you do?"

"Went back upriver and searched that whole section. That's when I discovered that dozens and dozens of bull caribou had drowned."

"Let me get this straight . . . every time you spotted a grizzly, you had to get close enough to see what it was eating on—that it wasn't me?"

"Soon as I saw the carcass had antlers, I was out of there."

"Still, that was crazy to keep looking."

"Hey, you're my brother."

I didn't know what to say about that, but I took it in, and it went deep. Would I have done the same?

"The pictures I could have taken, Nick! I could run this river a hundred times—or walk it—and never see the like."

I told Ryan that the mother grizzly with first-year cubs I had seen on a carcass was probably the same one he'd seen in battle with that big male later on. How much later, we would never know. On our separate sides of the river, both of us had slowed down for a couple of days trying to figure out where the other was. Then both of us, around the same time, decided to give it up and head for the coast.

Ryan said, "Have you found anything to eat since that char?"

"Not a thing."

"The way you caught it . . . was that something you learned from your grandfather?"

"No, from an episode of *Man vs. Wild.*"

He thought that was really funny. Seeing him laugh, I did too. Laughter was such a relief. Ryan said he wasn't sure I had heard him when he was shouting across the river just after the accident. He was trying to say how sorry he was about what happened. "I can't explain it," he said. "You heard Red Wiley, and I heard the same thing back at the park office: June fifteenth has always been the starting date for rafting on the Firth River. The winter ice is always gone by then. Maybe it had to do with extreme weather brought about by climate change. More snow than usual in that location, then a cooler spring?"

He noticed I was studying him closely.

"Don't get me wrong, Nick—that's no excuse. A boatman should never assume what's around the bend, even if he knows the river like the back of his hand. In the Grand Canyon, a debris flow down a side canyon can create a major rapid overnight. In forested country, trees might be blocking the river. This was driver error—all my fault. I could have got to shore in time if I hadn't turned my back to the river for the sake of a few photos of a swimming grizzly. Stupid, stupid, stupid—I won't call it an accident."

He's honest, I thought. That counts for a lot.

"I could've got us both killed."

"Close call, for sure."

"If only one of us had lived, and it was me, I would've never forgiven myself. I hope you'll forgive me."

"Done, Brother."

He reached out and clapped my shoulder. "Thanks—that's huge."

14

LIKE JONAH AND ME

"Let's go find our groceries," my brother said, and we headed downriver in search of the raft. Even if we didn't find it, I wasn't alone anymore, and not nearly as scared.

The walking would have been easy here, on the flats between the river and the foot of the mountains, if I wasn't so weak. Hunger was gnawing at my insides, and I was starting to go light-headed.

I was watching for animals. With trees so scarce this close to the ocean, they had no place to hide. *Open up your eyes*, I told myself. You're a hunter, bred to the bone, and you're in the middle of that "hunter's paradise" of

Jonah's. Find the caribou first, then worry how you're going to get one.

The only animals I managed to spot were Dall sheep, so high up and so far away, they looked like tiny white dots.

Another day done. With the midnight sun low in the valley ahead, Ryan said, "Let's rest for a while." I got down on the tundra, and it was lights-out within seconds. Four hours later I woke to Ryan chewing on a stem of cotton grass. I thought about asking if that did anything for his hunger, but I already knew the answer. Instead I asked if he'd gotten any sleep. He shook his head. I notched Day 7 on my knife sheath. We started out again.

Around nine in the morning I noticed a golden eagle flying a big circle above our side of the river. A short while later I spied a caribou with a calf on the flats about a quarter of a mile ahead of us.

As we got a little closer I noticed that the calf wasn't eating any grass, just nursing. Most calves are born right around June 1. This calf should be grazing by now, and it looked small, much too small, for June 21. This one was still wearing its reddish-brown birth coat. It might only be one week old.

This calf must have been born here in the Firth River

country. The calf's mother was a straggler who hadn't been able to keep up with the other cows as they migrated north to the calving grounds on the coastal plain. Jonah always said that without "safety in numbers" going for them, stragglers don't stand much of a chance.

All these things were going through my mind as I watched the caribou and her calf and the golden eagle. That eagle was circling a little lower. It wouldn't be long before the eagle made its move.

I was preparing to make mine. I told Ryan to hang back, that I was going to pick up the pace and try to get closer to the caribou. He looked quizzical but said, "Go for it."

I hurried forward, then slowed down as the eagle swung around. It flew another circle and I had time to get closer yet, to the cover of a lone spruce tree, without the caribou getting on to me. I kept my eye on the eagle.

The eagle descended into its strafing run. Like Red Wiley coming in for a landing, the great bird had its flaps down.

That golden eagle raked the back of the calf before the mother ever saw it coming. In the moment the calf cried out, I was tempted to start my own run but held off.

The calf was still on its feet, blood streaming from the open wounds along its back. The eagle beat its wings, gaining altitude for another pass.

At a week old, the calf was too big for the eagle to lift. The eagle was about to circle around and make another strike that would bring the calf down. I figured I should keep still. If I ran from cover now, it would be a mistake. Despite the loss of blood, the calf would probably out-run me.

The great bird wheeled around and dropped into its second strafing run. The desperate mother didn't know what was wrong with her bawling calf. By the time she spotted the approaching eagle, it was too late. Those slic-ing talons raked the calf's back again. I broke into a run as the eagle landed a short distance from the two caribou.

The bird ran and hopped toward the calf. The mother caribou came between them. She had dropped her ant-lers after calving, but her hooves were lethal weapons. As I closed in, I drew my hunting knife.

The mother caribou saw me for the first time, and she was in a quandary. She was successfully facing off the eagle, but now she had me to deal with. She bolted. Her calf, blood streaming down its sides, ran after her.

The eagle hissed at me. I threw up my arms, screamed and yelled, and the bird ran off, beating its wings until it was airborne. I chased the calf, wishing it didn't have this much strength left. Before long I ran it down. I ended its terror with my knife across its throat.

The calf's mother hadn't run far, and was watching it all. "I'm sorry," I said to her. To her calf I said, "Thank you."

By the time Ryan caught up with me I had the calf gutted. "Well done, Nick!"

I offered him the liver, told him he should start on that—it would be the easiest to keep down on an empty stomach. I ate the heart and one of the kidneys. Ryan ate the other kidney.

I had no stomach for eating the rest of the calf raw, but there wasn't any firewood close by. I draped the animal over my shoulders and we walked for another mile before we came to a tongue of spruce trees that came off a ridge to the edge of the valley floor. Within an hour we were roasting strips of caribou on sticks over a small fire. Ryan had the good sense not to overcook his.

That day rolled into the next, with us either eating or sleeping. We slept about as well as you can, curled up in a ball on the ground like animals. The eating was much better. We squatted on our haunches and ate bits of milk-fed caribou from the tips of our knives. "Like the Bushmen of the Kalahari Desert," Ryan said.

Like Jonah and me, I thought, many a time together out on the land.

15

YOU SEE WHAT I SEE?

When we had eaten every last morsel of that deliciously tender calf meat, we set out again. I felt a whole lot better, much stronger. Before long we saw more caribou, a small herd on a ridge ahead and to the right. It was rocky up there, nothing for caribou to eat. The windy ridges gave them relief from their bloodsucking tormentors. The coats of the calves up there shone silvery brown. They were about three weeks old. The coats of the cows were blotched with clumps of unshed winter fur.

As much as possible, we walked the rim of the canyon so we could keep the river in sight below. Ryan said our chances of finding the raft were improving. We were seeing more rocks in the river that rafts could get pinned on, huge rocks that had broken loose from the walls.

We were also seeing caribou, but only trickles of them. In the early hours of the next day a flood of caribou was approaching the canyon from the west. My photographer brother had no camera in his hands, but even so, he had a satisfied smile on his face. So did I. This was the most I'd ever laid eyes on.

I wondered where the herd would swim the river. Just to the north would be a good choice. On their side, no more than a hundred yards from us, a grassy chute led down to the river. Our side had no cliffs at all for half a mile.

The leaders must have remembered that chute from years gone by. They paused only seconds before starting down it. Behind them, the wide front of the herd flowed into the funneling chute toward the water. It was quite a crowd: the cows with their shabby-looking coats; their calves, looking awfully small to swim this river; the yearling bulls that had migrated to the calving grounds with the females; and the recently arrived mature bulls with their big racks and magnificent new coats, white as snow on their manes and chests.

The leaders stopped at the shore, sizing up the crossing. They hesitated, anxious and unsure, while more and more animals came surging down the chute, so many that the crush from behind left the leaders no choice. They took the plunge.

The rest followed without hesitation, leaping into the water. Lit by the radiant Arctic light, soft and golden, caribou soon filled the river from shore to shore, from the small but sturdy calves to the biggest bulls with their bristling antlers. It was something to see.

It took a good while for the caribou to cross, at least fifteen hundred, we guessed. When the last of them climbed out of the river on our side, we stayed put to watch the big flow of animals browse its way across the broad tundra bench and onto the flanks of the treeless mountains. "Sure wish you had your camera," I said.

Ryan waved the mosquitoes from his face. "Even if I don't get a chance to take pictures, what I just saw was worth the price of admission."

"How many caribou did you see last summer on that other Arctic trip you did?"

"No more than sixty."

"What river were you on?"

"The Burnside, in Canada's central Arctic. I was expecting to see huge numbers of caribou. The Bathurst herd has always been a big one. The last time the wildlife people had done an aerial survey—ten years before— they counted over four hundred thousand. I got back home, and a couple of months later I found out that a new aerial survey had been conducted shortly after I was there. After studying all the photographs, the total count was thirty-four thousand."

This news landed like a stunning blow, and I was slow to speak. "I didn't know it was that bad. All we heard was that the government put quotas on caribou for the Inuit and the Indians over there. That's unheard-of! Over here we can still take all the caribou we need."

"If you don't mind me asking, how many do you personally get in a year?"

"Usually around twenty-five, almost all of them in the fall when they're still on the tundra but migrating south toward the trees. It takes that many to feed us and the relatives and friends who can't hunt for themselves. We make it last all winter. If we had to live on a quota of a few caribou a year, it would be a disaster."

"From what I hear, the team of caribou experts from the Yukon Territory and Alaska haven't been able to do their photographic survey of the Porcupine herd since 2001. For the last nine years, they've had weather problems, or smoke from distant forest fires, and some summers the caribou don't form into the large groups that make a census possible. If I remember correctly, the 2001 count was one hundred and twenty thousand caribou, down from one hundred and eighty thousand in

1989. If that steady decline has continued since 2001 . . .
What have you been hearing, Nick?"

"They're afraid the herd might be down to a hundred thousand or even ninety by now. We think there's more, but after what you said about the Bathurst herd, I'm really worried. What if there's even fewer than the government thinks?"

Ryan didn't say, but I could hear what he was thinking: we'd be facing quotas, too.

We set off again, soon walking across the stretch of ground where the herd had just been. Soaked with urine, it sure smelled gamey. The tundra was freshly grazed and littered with droppings. Ryan was amazed by the numbers of robins we were seeing. I told him they used to be an unusual sight, according to Jonah. "Even in my lifetime," I added, "I see more red foxes and fewer Arctic foxes. And get this: Pacific salmon are showing up in our nets out at Shingle Point."

"Birds, animals, and fish all moving north," Ryan said. "Great climate-change observations for my article. What if, in the future, it warms up enough for the trees to move north all the way to the ocean, and there's no more open tundra? Would the land support very many caribou?"

"Don't even go there," I said. "I never heard that one. That blows my mind."

Next time the canyon walls tailed off and we were able to walk along the shore for a while, we discovered that the water in the Firth was still dropping. The falling river had left a thick high-tide line of caribou hair along the shore. The cows had shed gobs of their shaggy winter coats as they swam the river.

Pretty quick the Firth was back in its canyon again, and the walls were the highest yet, more than a hundred feet. A pair of rough-legged hawks flew back and forth screaming at us. "They must have a nest nearby," Ryan said. That was pretty sharp of him. Rough-legged hawks don't like it a bit when people are anywhere near their nests.

We spotted their nest and moved on. Before long we had a lot more rough-legged hawks giving us what-for. Over the span of an hour we spotted thirteen nests on the west side of the river. There were probably as many on our side underneath the edge of the cliff.

The parent hawks were bringing rodents to their young, mostly ground squirrels and lemmings. Across the river, one nest wasn't being guarded; maybe both of the adults were away hunting. We weren't the only ones to notice. A red fox was climbing the cliff underneath it, carefully yet steadily finding a way up among the cracks and ledges. No doubt the fox had young of its own to feed. Even so, I was amazed at the risk the fox was taking. I thought for sure it would give up, but I was wrong. The fox made it all the way up, nabbed a fledgling, and was halfway down when one of the parents returned, screaming mad. The hawk dive-bombed the fox with raking talons. Fox and fledgling fell to their deaths.

We'd been so absorbed with what we were seeing across the river, neither of us had looked into the distance downstream. I did, just as we were turning to go. I saw white water down there, a major rapid where the river was turning a bend. Something unnatural in the rapid caught my eye, a patch of bright blue.

Pointing, I said to Ryan, "Check out that rapid. You see what I see?"

"The raft!" he cried.

It was out in the river, hung up on a boulder.

"We'll never be able to get to it out there," I said.

Ryan wasn't saying anything. "Can't tell yet," he said finally.

Half an hour later we were looking down on the raft from the cliff directly above it. There's no way, I thought. Situation hopeless.

Even though the raft was only thirty feet from shore, it was folded around the leading edge of a huge boulder shaped like the prow of a ship. To make things worse, the boulder sat at the foot of the rapid. White water was boiling off it.

"It's wrapped," Ryan said grimly. "A wrap is worse than a flip. One of the tubes is deflated . . . one of the spare oars got ripped off the side of the raft . . . it's hard to tell if all the gear survived the ride. Let's hope everything's there, especially my hard-shell camera box!"

A couple hundred yards north, a break in the cliffs allowed us to get down to the shore and scramble upstream to the foot of the rapid. I still thought the recovery of even one little metal box—preferably the one with the satellite phone—was out of the question. My hopes rose when Ryan said he had helped recover rafts wrapped around boulders in the Grand Canyon.

"I don't see much gear," I said.

"That's because it's underwater. The cargo net appears to be intact. This might not be as bad as it looks."

If you say so, I thought.

Ryan was able to swim to the raft. At the spot where the current was least powerful, he pulled himself onto one of the raft tubes, then higher onto the flat top of the boulder. I had no idea he was that strong. The caribou meat he had recently eaten gets some of the credit, I'm sure.

From his perch on the boulder, Ryan was able to climb onto the pinned raft. He went after rope and carabiners first. He was hoping to rig a pulley system to ferry the gear bit by bit to the shore. While getting hit with freezing white water, he retrieved the one-hundred-foot coil of climbing rope he had brought along, with carabiners clipped to it. He had prepared for an emergency like the one we were looking at.

Ryan rigged his pulley system between the boat and the shore. Setting it up took several more swims on his part. I waded halfway to the raft when he was ready. Out at the raft, he grabbed hold of the gear and clipped it to "prussic knots" he had attached to the rope. I stood in shallow water heaving on the rope hand over hand. The first item I brought to shore was the ammo can with the first aid. The second was the can with the satellite phone. Ryan hollered over the sound of the rapid, "Open it up and see if the phone stayed dry!"

Heart in my throat, I did, and hollered back, "Not a drop!"

The third item I hauled to shore was Ryan's hard-shell camera box. "Want me to open it?" I yelled.

"Might as well find out now!"

His two cameras and his extra lenses were nestled in foam just like he'd left them. Same for the memory cards and the rest of his camera stuff. "Dry as a bone!" I reported.

My brother let out a victory whoop that might've

carried to Herschel Island, if anyone was listening.

Some of our vinyl river bags had stayed sealed, others not. No big deal. Clothing would dry fast with round-the-clock sunshine and wind.

Here came my day bag with sunglasses, sunscreen, lip balm, bug repellent, energy bars, and more.

The big white cooler was heavier than it should have been, and no wonder. The river had gotten inside. All that fresh food meant for the first week was spoiled. Oh well, the first week was history anyway.

After every few minutes in the water, we had to recuperate, Ryan atop the boulder and me on a slab of rock beside the river. The last item to come ashore was the raft itself. It felt like the two of us were hauling in a whale. No wonder one of the raft's four perimeter tubes had deflated—it had a six-inch rip in it.

At the foot of the cliffs there wasn't a flat spot large enough for Ryan to do the repair. We had to roll the raft up and carry it out the same as everything else. Where the cliffs tailed into the river, we humped all the gear up to the first grassy spot that would serve as a campsite. We were both worse than spent.

My eyes bugged out at the sight of all the canned and packaged food in the larger ammunition boxes, all undamaged and watertight. Our tent bag was dry, and so was Ryan's big river bag with his sleeping bag and personal stuff. Mine had taken water. I hadn't folded the top with as many wraps as Ryan had said. I spread everything out to dry.

The wind died suddenly. Out of the tundra came the mosquitoes. Out of my day bag came my bug shirt, and over my head it went. I threw up the hood and zipped the netting shut across my neck. How sweet it was, and what a good feeling to have some bear protection again—my pouch of bear bangers, our backup can of pepper spray, and the air horn.

This was the first I'd laid eyes on the air horn. It looked like a can of soda with a dinky red trumpet mounted on top, and it came with a holster for wearing on your hip. "Does it work?" I asked.

Ryan shrugged. "Some say yes, some say no."

We put camp together, tables and chairs and cooking gear and all. After a supper of chili and corn bread—chili cooked on the propane stove and corn bread baked over charcoal in a Dutch oven—we crawled into the tent. I was so tired I didn't even waste the lung power to inflate my ground pad. I just rolled it out, unzipped my sleeping bag and got in, grabbed my fleece jacket for a pillow, and crashed like a fighter plane going down in the sea.

16

INSIDE INFORMATION

After thirteen hours of sleep I crawled out of the tent. It was ten in the morning, and the wind was blowing strong enough to keep the bugs down. Over a breakfast of pancakes, fried Spam, and oatmeal with peaches, I found out that my brother had been up for hours. He had already sewn up the rip in the raft tube and glued a patch over it.

I asked Ryan if he'd seen any caribou moving through. He hadn't. I said, "Maybe that herd swimming the river was the biggest bunch we'll see."

My brother feigned horror. "Now that I've got my cameras? Tell me that it isn't so!"

I wasn't sure what to tell him. If he knew how vast

the range of the Porcupine herd was, he would know he didn't stand much of a chance. Granted, they weren't in their winter range in the trees down south in the Porcupine River country, but their summer range was vast in itself.

"Jonah saw big numbers once, really big numbers, here in the Firth country, but he was lucky."

Ryan winked and said, "I brought along a secret weapon. Actually, two."

"Really? What are they?"

"Our satellite phone and our handheld GPS."

"Where do those get you?"

"To the post-calving aggregation, I hope. That's what the caribou biologists call the phenomenon when lots of smaller herds gather into herds numbering in the tens of thousands. When it happens, it's usually about a month after calving."

"That's what Jonah must have seen, but how do a phone and a GPS get you there?"

"Here's how. The Canadian and American caribou biologists who study the Porcupine herd have put satellite collars on a hundred and twenty cows. The location of each one can be pinpointed day or night by the twenty-four satellites that make up the Global Positioning System. Keep in mind that each of those collared caribou represents about one thousand that aren't collared."

"Our hunters know all about that. It's on a government website. We used to be able to track the caribou on our computers. Then they made it so you could only see where the caribou were in past years."

"So you couldn't use it as a hunting tool."

"Right."

"Did you, before they pulled it?"

"Me and Jonah, no, because Jonah is against putting satellite collars on the animals—bears, caribou, whatever. So we never took advantage."

"Did other hunters take advantage?"

"Some did. Who's to blame them? They were trying to feed their families."

"Sounds like you don't always agree with your grandfather."

"Of course not. As I tried to explain to him, tracking caribou with your laptop was just the newest tool, like rifles taking the place of spears. Anyway, it didn't last long. Nobody was surprised when the government quit showing where the caribou were. So how can you track the . . . wait a second . . . do you have some kind of inside information?"

Ryan's dark beard parted with a wide smile. "Yep, I've got a friend who's a caribou biologist. Lives in Whitehorse. Ken Logan has been studying the Porcupine herd for a dozen years or more. He even spent five months following them on the ground once. Here's the plan: I call him up on the sat phone, he calls up a bookmark on his computer—at the office or at home—and he's looking at the present location of those hundred and twenty dots we were just talking about, superimposed over a map of northeast Alaska and the Yukon Territory of Canada."

"He tells you if a bunch of the dots are coming together—if the mother of all herds is gathering—and you hike to that location?"

"Steering by my GPS," he agreed with a nod and a smile.

"I bet you checked in with him this morning. What did he say? Are the caribou gathering?"

My brother surprised me with a shrug. "I didn't call."

"Why not? That's what you came for."

"I'm not in a rush."

I put my coffee down. "After ten days, and what we've been through, you aren't in a rush?"

Ryan took a long sip from his mug. "It's a matter of first things first."

"Like what?"

"I'm waiting on your feelings about where we stand."

"My feelings? I don't get it."

"Okay, I'll spit it out. After everything you've been through, you might want to think of putting the pedal to the metal tomorrow."

"Meaning what?"

"We could reach the coast in a couple of days. By tomorrow afternoon we would be close enough to put in the call to Red."

"You'd give up on finding the caribou and taking your pictures?"

Ryan looked me square in the eye. "That's not nearly as important to me as you are. After what I've put you through, I am highly motivated to get you home safe and sound."

For a second I was about to jump in and agree with him. Here was the chance to get home soon and in one piece after all that hardship. My natural instinct, though, was to hold back and think about it. Strange to say, I hadn't even thought of quitting. Since we'd gotten the raft back, I'd assumed we were going to chase after the caribou.

I sat there letting this soak in. The sooner I got home, the better my chances of seeing my grandfather before he slipped away. I pictured what that would be like. Jonah would ask, "Did you see caribou far as your eye could see?" I would have to say, "No, Jonah, we had some trouble. We had to give it up, didn't really try. . . ."

That was hardly the good-bye I'd been picturing. And I really did believe Jonah when he said he'd be there when I got back, that he wasn't ready to make his last journey just yet. My brother and I had plenty of food, and nobody was expecting us anytime soon. July 15 was the date Ryan and Red had agreed on for Red to pick us up on the shore of the Beaufort Sea. July 15 was a long ways off—twenty-one days.

But did it really make sense to patch up the trip after it had started so badly? To go out on the land, for who knew how long, after we'd lost more than half of our bear protection, such as it was? We'd already had more than a lifetime's worth of bear trouble on this trip . . . wasn't it crazy to risk even more?

Here was another thing that argued for calling it quits. Even if we did find the mother of all herds, how was Jonah going to feel about the way we did it? He was going to ask how we tracked the caribou, the signs on the land that we followed.

I decided to spit it out. I said, "Jonah wouldn't like the idea of us tracking caribou that have been chased by helicopters into nets and then tranquilized. Give me an example that would convince him it's okay for those government experts to put satellite collars on the caribou."

"Fair enough. You can tell him some of the things the caribou biologists have learned about the Porcupine caribou using these methods. For starters, they've found out that two-thirds of the calves are born on the Alaska side of the coastal plain. Only one-third are born on the Canadian side."

"We already knew that. Like Jonah always says, just ask the old hunters."

"Well, you know how it is, the science guys are all about data and facts. They set out to learn why the caribou calve more on the Alaska side. Part of that involved studying the survival rate of calves born to collared mothers on the Alaska side compared to those on the Canadian side. Get this: calves born on the Alaska side survive more often than calves born on the Canadian side."

"Never heard that. How come?"

"Here's what seems to be the answer. The forage that produces the most nutritious milk—cotton grass—grows more abundantly on the Alaska portion of the calving grounds. Thanks to cotton grass, caribou milk has the highest fat content of any land mammal."

"Cool. I didn't know that."

"Here's something else about the Alaska side of the calving grounds: there's fewer predators over there. The land is too flat and wet for wolves to make their dens. The wolves have to stay within reach of their dens to be able to feed their young."

"Okay, but how does knowing all that change anything?"

"Well, the calving grounds on the Canadian side lie

within Ivvavik National Park, which was created to permanently protect them."

"Sure, that's why we agreed to the park. Ivvavik means 'birthing place' in our language."

"Here's the rub. On the Alaska side, the calving grounds don't have permanent protection."

"Why not?"

"When the Arctic National Wildlife Refuge was created back in 1980, oil had already been discovered underneath the strip of coastal plain where the caribou drop their calves. Congress postponed the decision whether to develop that small piece of the overall refuge for oil or protect it for the caribou. The way it stands today, it's still up to which way the political winds are blowing."

"That's not right. What kind of wildlife refuge is that?"

"It is what it is, and it comes up for a vote every few years. It's a squeaker every time. The pro-development senators show pictures of caribou grazing in front of pipelines, and claim you can take the oil out without harming the caribou. They never mention the studies done by the American and Canadian caribou biologists. Maybe they don't even look at them."

"What do the studies say?"

"That caribou can tolerate a certain amount of development where they graze, but none on their calving grounds. If their birthing place becomes an oil field, the Porcupine caribou herd would likely collapse."

"You're going to put all of that in your *National Geographic* article?"

"For sure. *National Geographic* has eight and a half million subscribers. A new article about the Porcupine herd and those caribou studies will help, no doubt about it."

"People way down there actually care?"

"They don't want the caribou to go the way of the buffalo. That's why I'm after the photos, to show that the caribou still roam in vast numbers, and are worth saving. And if I can put a human face on the subject by featuring Aklavik as one of the thirteen Native communities in Canada and Alaska that depend on the caribou, people will have even more reason to care."

So much for thinking that my brother wouldn't be able to write about the caribou and us. He must've spent no end of time learning all this stuff before he came up here. So much for thinking he had to be a hunter to care about hunters.

Now I knew. Ryan and I—Jonah, too—were all on the same side. "Call Whitehorse," I said.

17

HOT ON THEIR TRAIL

I jumped up and went for the sat phone. It was a clunker, nothing like a cell phone. "Call Whitehorse, Ryan. Right now. Let's find out if the dots are coming together."

"Only if you're going to sleep on it tonight, whatever we find out. I don't want you passing up the chance to head straight home without thinking it through."

"Deal. Let's make the call."

Ryan put the sat phone on speaker so I could follow the conversation. His friend the caribou biologist picked up. Ken Logan was surprised that Ryan hadn't checked in earlier. "Thought you might have had some trouble."

"We did," Ryan agreed. "Long story. We're fine now."

"Glad to hear it. What's your present location?"

Ryan gave him our GPS coordinates, adding that the river map showed us just upstream of Surprise Rapid and Big Bend Roller Coaster.

"I was thinking of you yesterday," Logan said. "My computer monitor showed two of our collared caribou about to cross the Firth, heading east. Wondered if you might be in position to photograph a pretty good mess of caribou as they swam the river. I left a message with the GPS coordinates on your sat phone."

"We weren't checking our messages. We happened to be there, though. Saw fifteen hundred or so."

"Good deal. Since then, lots of dots have been crossing the river downstream of your current position."

"Heading which way?"

"East, toward the Babbage River."

"Where were most of the calves born this year?"

"Typical year. Two-thirds were born on the Alaska side of the coastal plain, one-third on the coastal plain in Ivvavik National Park."

"About those dots that have been crossing the river—how many?"

"Twenty-seven dots, with more on the way. After they swam the river, they fanned out to the north and south, but now it looks like there might be a convergence in the foothills of the British Mountains, north and east of you. You might be in a position to photograph the biggest post-calving aggregation since 2001."

"How far should we take the raft downriver before we start walking?"

"Ten miles, no more."

"Then how far east?"

"Twenty-five miles, maybe—depends on what they do. You're in for some hoofing for sure. Stay in touch. I'll be tracking them from home as well as the office. Does your GPS have the maps of the Yukon Territory's north slope?"

"Yes, and photo view as well."

"Excellent. I'll send you there like a guided missile."

They arranged for Ryan to call from ten miles down the river. Soon as my brother switched off, he got out his river guide and turned to the map with the stretch of the canyon we were in. He showed me where we were, then pointed out a campsite down the river at Canyon Creek. "We could get there today," I said, "if we really got with it. I'll sleep on it there, okay?"

"Canyon Creek it is. Did you want to call home, let them know you're okay?"

"It's expensive, isn't it?"

"Yes, but don't even think about that."

"They're not expecting me to call . . . no, I don't want to. I might find out something I don't want to know."

With that we turned to doing the dishes and breaking down camp. We carried the raft to the river, pumped it up, and strapped on the frame. It took another hour to load and rig the gear. Around three in the afternoon, after nine days without the raft, we launched back onto the river.

Surprise Rapid was waiting just around the bend. Our rain gear saved us a drenching from the ice water that cascaded inside the raft. All I had to do was hang on. Without a lick of trouble, Ryan took us through Surprise and all the way through Big Bend Roller Coaster, which was two miles long. Turns out he knew how to row a white-water raft after all. We pulled into the mouth of Canyon Creek, set up camp, and made supper.

Crawling into my sleeping bag that night, I thought about that decision I had to make, but not for long. I was dead asleep in a minute or two.

I woke a little after six in the morning to the smell of coffee. I crawled out of the tent and Ryan poured me a cup. "I'm in," I said. "I wanna see those caribou, and I want you to get your pictures."

"Good deal," he said. "Thank you."

After breakfast we climbed to the rim of the canyon to

use the sat phone. Ryan called his friend in Whitehorse. More and more dots were coming together on Ken Logan's monitor—more than thirty thousand caribou!

Under heavy backpacks that morning of Day 11, we paused on the shoulder of the ridge above Canyon Creek to take in a last glimpse of the gear we were leaving behind. Ryan had been extra cautious, deflating the boat and rolling it up for fear of high winds or a bear having a bad day. After that we carried the boat, frame, and everything else up the slope to a spot out of reach of Noah's flood.

Ryan left a note in an empty jar that said who we were. He dated it June 25. Ryan brought out his second camera, gave me a few instructions, and hung it around my neck. I told him I wasn't very big on taking pictures.

We turned away from the Firth River and dropped into a wide green valley without a single tree. Ryan stopped now and again to take pictures of the expanse of rolling tundra. He was keeping his GPS handy in his shirt pocket, and scrolled the map every so often to update our exact position. After a couple of hours we stopped to rest and eat. Ryan called Ken to see if we were still headed in the right direction. Here's the first thing the biologist said: "Bet you guys have the hoods of your bug shirts zipped up."

"That we do," Ryan said. "But how'd you know?"

"Because those dots on my computer monitor have scattered. Looks like the caribou stampeded out of the foothills to get away from the bugs. Climbed onto the high ridges where the wind is blowing."

"I hope this doesn't mean the weather is going to put an end to the post-calving aggregation."

"There's hope in the forecast. There's a storm brewing in the northern Pacific, and some of the models show it heading across Alaska and onto the north slope of the Yukon Territory. If it even brushes the north slope, you'll get plenty enough wind to keep the bugs grounded. The caribou will come down off the ridges to feed and have their big reunion."

Ryan gave his friend our coordinates, and mentioned that we'd been seeing a lot of fresh caribou scat. He wondered if there were any dots close to our present location.

"You bet. Six, pretty well clumped. Got your pencil ready?"

Ryan jotted down the coordinates we needed to be able to steer toward those six dots. We marched on. My pack wasn't nearly as heavy as my brother's, but it felt as heavy as the load of caribou meat I had carried on my back six weeks before, on the day the grolar bear surprised me on the bank of the Mackenzie. Ryan and I were carrying food for nine days, a backpacking stove and plenty of fuel, his heavy camera gear, our tent, sleeping bags and ground pads, and enough clothes to weather a snowstorm.

Steering east according to Ken Logan's directions, we followed a newly trampled caribou trail through a low pass. We dropped into a basin where we came across a caribou highway two feet wide cut into the dark earth. It was flanked by minor trails on both sides. Caribou like to follow one behind the other, moving in parallel lines. A big herd has dozens of leaders and cuts dozens of trails. We were walking in the wake of a very large herd that had passed this way only hours before. The tundra was littered with fresh droppings, and the air was sharp from dark spots of urine that hadn't yet evaporated.

We followed the caribou highway back and forth across a creek, climbing all the while. I almost bumped into my brother when he stopped dead in his tracks. I stepped to the side to see what he was looking at: two stragglers, a cow with her calf.

The cow was no more than a hundred feet away, facing our direction, but didn't seem to see us. She was sneezing and shaking her head. Her legs were splayed; she barely had the strength to stand. Her head was down, and thick strands of dark snot were hanging from her snout. Her calf, alert and healthy, was grazing about twenty feet away.

The mother caribou was engulfed in a swarm of

botflies. I've always hated bots with a passion. They're about the size of houseflies, but they're more like wasps. They lay their eggs in the nostrils of the caribou, and the larvae grow by the hundreds and thousands in the animal's sinus cavities and lungs. The bot swarm we were looking at wasn't the first to get at this caribou. She was so far gone, she was already blind.

Ryan was taking pictures as the mother caribou went down. She tried to rise but didn't have the strength. As her calf came to her, Ryan took more pictures. We didn't stay to see the end of the story. Ravens would come down to feed as soon as the mother was dead, possibly before. Scavengers watching the ravens would soon follow—a wolf or a bear, maybe a wolverine. By the next day there would be nothing left of cow and calf but bones and hide.

We kept to the caribou trails we'd been following, up the creek and all the way up a tongue of tundra that ended at the foot of a rocky slope. When we looked up we saw hundreds of caribou lining the ridges. Ryan got out his telephoto lens and took some pictures of them silhouetted against the blue sky.

We made another bunch of miles before we stopped for the night on the far shore of a river shallow enough to wade. Ryan called Whitehorse. Ken said that the concentration of dots we'd thought we were gaining on had picked up the pace and moved twenty to thirty miles that day, east through the foothills. We would have to cover a lot of ground the next day to stay within striking distance.

In the middle of the night I was wakened by the clicking of caribou tendons. I had never heard the clicks this close. It was just after three in the morning, bright as day of course. The wind was fluttering the tent. Through the yellow fabric I saw that we were surrounded by caribou. A bull with a trophy rack was grazing on Ryan's side of the tent. I reached for the camera he'd given me and turned it on. I switched it to automatic like he had shown me and snapped the silhouette of the long-snouted head and wide, branching antlers.

The sound of the shutter didn't disturb the caribou but woke Ryan up like I was hoping. He looked at me groggily. "Caribou," I whispered, "all around us." Ryan wormed his way out of his sleeping bag. Quietly as possible, he opened the netting door and crawled outside with his camera. The caribou didn't spook. When my brother came back into the tent half an hour later, he said he'd taken pictures of the herd passing through camp, with our tent like a boulder in the middle of a river.

We went back to sleep, and by the time we got up, they had vanished. A bear showed up as we were eating breakfast. I spotted it at half a mile, headed our direction. Most likely it was following the herd, but we might have brought it on ourselves. Hiking in the heat all this time had left us pretty rank. "Here comes trouble," I said. "Big old grizzly."

18

THEY JUST DON'T GET IT

The grizzly was a big male with a frosty-brown face and forelegs. The rest of its body was dark brown. The bear stopped running at a hundred yards. It stood on its hind feet for a better look. "Get your bear bangers ready," Ryan said as he snapped pictures. I had already taken the launcher and three cartridges from the pouch on my belt. "Got one loaded," I said, "and two in my shirt pocket."

I reminded Ryan that our air horn and pepper spray were clipped to his belt. Ryan kept the air horn, but handed off the spray. "This is for point-blank range," he reminded me.

"I know. What about the bear bangers?"

"Before the bear charges . . . whenever you think he's getting too close."

I clipped the pepper-spray holster to my belt while keeping an eye on the bear. It had all fours back on the ground and was loping toward us. At fifty yards it stood up again, woofed a couple of times, then laid back its ears and clacked its teeth. Now was the time. I took the safety off the launcher, pointed it above the bear, and fired.

The whistling sound of the speeding banger was weird to begin with. When the thing exploded above the bear like a rifle blast, that grizzly came to ground, uncertain whether to charge or flee. Fast as I could, I loaded another cartridge and fired again. At the second blast, the grizzly took off like an Arctic hare.

That grizzly covered a lot of ground in a hurry. A couple of minutes later it disappeared into the folds of the land about a mile away.

I was all pumped up. "You see that thing run?"

"Fast as a racehorse! I got some great pictures."

A couple hours after setting out again, we caught sight of a caribou herd, maybe the same one Ryan had photographed in the middle of the night. From the cover of boulders on a knoll, Ryan took pictures of a wolf parting the herd. The wolf was scouting the caribou for prey—an old one, a sick one, a calf with a gimpy leg. As big as they come, the wolf was the spitting image of that white wolf that kept me company on the banks of the Firth.

The caribou weren't running from the wolf—not yet. And the wolf wasn't going to give chase until the time was right.

Suddenly the wolf locked on to a victim, and broke into a run. In that instant, a thousand caribou took off like the wind.

It was a thing to see. The white wolf was running alongside hundreds of caribou. In a matter of seconds it sprinted between a mother and her calf. In turning away from the wolf, the calf was isolated from the herd, and was running for its life all on its lonesome.

The rest of the caribou stopped running as soon as they realized the wolf wasn't after them. They watched as the calf ran a big circle away from the herd and back toward it, with the wolf sprinting all out no more than twenty feet behind. "Would you look at that," Ryan said under his breath, eye to the viewfinder with his shutter whirring in motor drive.

Fast as the wolf could run, the month-old calf could run even faster. There wasn't a thing wrong with it. The calf was winning its race for survival, but in a flash it stumbled on loose rock and went down. The wolf struck before it had time to rise, and had it by the neck, and gave the calf a killing bite. The only time I'd seen this before was on a video at school.

The stumble, and the end of the chase, happened no more than fifty yards away from our vantage point in those boulders on the knoll. Ryan had his camera on motor drive as the wolf caught up with the calf. He showed me the close-ups, *National Geographic* quality for sure.

That evening we came to the banks of a shallow river in the foothills of the mountains. The weather was changing. The sky was full of high clouds and the wind was blowing harder than before. We decided not to wait until morning to ford the river. On the east bank we set up camp and made supper. After we ate, Ryan made his call to Ken and reported our location. The biologist was out-of-his-mind excited. He said the dots were coming together for us, more than he ever expected—thirty-nine dots, a third of the Porcupine herd's estimated strength.

"Forty thousand caribou!" Ryan exclaimed. "When? How soon?"

"Maybe as early as tomorrow."

"Where?"

"Babbage River valley, your side of the river, fifteen miles from your present position. You and your brother are right on the money, Ryan."

"We've got high clouds and wind. What's the forecast say?"

"That Alaska system is still offshore and building up steam. It threw out a band of moisture that might reach you in a day or two. If the system tracks your way, a storm will probably arrive a couple days after that. You've got time to get your pictures, and right now, the caribou have no reason to head for the hills."

"Good deal! Good deal all around!"

"You bet. Everything's favorable for the first aerial census in nine years. It got started today, four planes with cameras on their bellies. They'll be doing photographic transects over the Arctic National Wildlife Refuge and the north slope of the Yukon Territory. They key on the collared caribou first, then eyeball the terrain for the rest. Get close to the caribou, you'll get your picture taken!"

"We'll wave."

"There's one other thing, Ryan."

"What's that?"

"Just a curiosity, but something to keep in mind. I've also been tracking a freak of nature, a bear that's half polar bear, half barren-ground grizzly. You might have heard of it back in Inuvik."

"Sure did, and my brother's the one who tangled with it."

"How about that! Tell him there's been a second sighting."

"Where?"

"Foothills of the Richardson Mountains, south and west of Aklavik."

"When?"

"Thirteen days ago."

"You say you've been tracking it. How can that be?"

"Roger McKeon, the polar bear expert, tranquilized it from a helicopter. He put a satellite collar on the creature—a big male—and estimated its weight at around a thousand pounds. That's bigger than any barren-ground grizzly, big as a trophy polar bear!"

I couldn't believe what I was hearing. "He should've killed it," I muttered.

Ryan asked for the grolar bear's present location. Logan said it was on the coast, halfway between Shingle Point and King Point.

Ryan saw me scowling, and said into the phone, "A bear can cover a lot of ground in a hurry."

"Well, that's why I mentioned it. What can I say, other than heads up? I would think that your chances of running into it are remote. Good luck with the caribou tomorrow!"

Ken Logan gave us the coordinates for the grolar bear's exact location. My brother shrugged as he put the phone away. "Well, that was unsettling. Let's break out the GPS and find out how far away that grolar bear is."

I sure didn't think much of the answer: fifty-three miles. "I tried to warn them. They just don't get it. They haven't seen the look in its eyes. I can't believe they put a collar on it and let it go."

"Roger McKeon thinks it's a creature of climate change. As a scientist, he must want to learn everything about it that he can."

"Okay, but while he's doing science, somebody's going to get killed."

I didn't get much sleep that night. I was back on the banks of the Mackenzie River, facing that monster.

19

WALKING WITH CARIBOU

In the morning I notched Day 13 onto my knife sheath. Ryan called Whitehorse after breakfast. The megaherd was no longer along the Babbage River. During the night the caribou had moved farther east through the foothills. At the Trail River the dots turned south, tracking upstream into the mountains. Ken Logan gave us new coordinates to steer for.

My brother said it was time to make our move and intercept the caribou. We were going to climb between two mountains and drop into the headwaters of the Trail River from above.

As we began our march, a bush plane flew directly over us, only a few thousand feet up. We waved, and we joked about whether we'd be noticed by the caribou counters poring over the photographs.

Under heavy packs, the hiking was steep and strenuous. I kept my mind off it by imagining what we might see once we got there. Picturing huge numbers of caribou brought bears to mind—bears would be there too—and before long I was imagining us running into that freak of nature with features of grizzly and polar bear, and a patchwork coat. We'd better hope the grolar bear didn't catch wind of all those caribou.

Suddenly I recalled the smell of that bear, and the smell of my fear. My mind lurched southeast, in the direction of safety and home. Aklavik lay a hundred and fifty miles or more across the trackless tundra. On the verge of tears, I got ahold of myself and steered my thoughts back to the here and now, and our quest for the "post-calving aggregation." The ground we were walking was freshly grazed and trampled by their large split hooves. We huffed our way up the steep slope onto lichen-covered boulders with patches of bearberry among the rocks.

At the top of the pass, the ground leveled out. Two boulders rose from a wide patch of tundra. We propped our packs against the boulders, drank from our water bottles, ate energy bars, and stretched out on the grass for a nap.

I woke to the sound of my brother rummaging in his

pack. He was getting out his mini tripod. He pointed back down toward the rocky foot of the pass. Three different streams of caribou, maybe as many as a couple thousand, were headed our way. The clicking of their foot tendons carried up the mountainside, sounding uncannily close.

As the leaders drew near, we didn't make any attempt to hide. We sat atop the boulders about five feet above the grass. At twenty yards, the leaders took us in with their large brown eyes. They hesitated, then kept coming, some huffing, some snorting, some sneezing, some coughing, nearly all of them twitching their muscles to try to shake the mosquitoes from their bodies. The swarm of bugs following the herd reached us before the caribou did.

On came the caribou, their nostrils whooshing for breath, their long-suffering eyes rolling our way—those who even noticed. The flood of bodies and antlers was upon us. Ryan's shutter was whirring. I didn't take a single picture. At a time like this, I didn't want to be looking through a camera.

They were coming so close I could barely believe it. Their snorts, grunts, huffs, and wheezes filled my ears. My eyes took in their long snouts and rubbery noses, their white chest ruffs, the scars on their forelegs, their quivering muscles, their deep-brown shoulders and rumps. The branching racks of the big bulls were all in velvet. The calves were sturdy and full of spunk. Some tried to nurse as the herd passed through the bottleneck. Some called to their mothers; some snatched at sedges and lichen.

It took a good while for them all to come through the pass. By then the wind was blowing hard and the bugs had gone to ground. Clouds lower and thicker than the day before were racing in from the west. We followed the caribou down the other side of the mountain.

By the time we reached the valley of the Trail River, our herd had turned upstream and vanished. We followed, heading south. Before long we had another herd coming from behind. Every time I glanced over my shoulder, they were closer. Before long they were practically on our heels. I could hear their nostrils whooshing over my shoulder. My brother and I exchanged glances without saying a word. "*Unreal*," he mouthed.

Half a minute later they drew even with us, and we were walking with caribou. I had to tell myself this was really happening. Some of the caribou rolled their eyes at us as they passed by, but mostly they ignored us. We weren't hunters, and they weren't prey. It was like we were seeing each other in a dream. I touched the back of a calf and felt its spine run under my palm. "Grow big and strong," I murmured. "Make more caribou."

After that herd passed us by, we didn't see any more

for a while. We kept following the Trail River upstream. Mostly the river was slow and winding, with chest-high willows lining its banks. In spots it ran fast through the riffles. It was loaded with grayling.

Rounding a bend, we climbed to the top of a small, flat-topped hill that rose all alone from the floor of the widening valley. With nary a tree in sight, we could see a long, long way. Our eyes were greeted by the vision we'd come for. Upstream, the valley floor was teeming with caribou, and so were the lower slopes of the surrounding mountains. "Huge numbers!" my brother declared.

"Tens of thousands! Should we try to get closer?"

"We've got high ground here—a perfect place to shoot from. Let's stay put, and hope they come to us."

Ryan walked over to a circle of stones, ten or so feet in diameter, at the very center of the hilltop. "Got any idea what these are about?"

I was proud to say that I did. "Prehistoric tent circle. The stones held down the edges of the caribou hides."

"Very cool," Ryan said as he snapped away. We pitched our tent inside that ring where my ancestors had tented every time they came here to hunt. It must have been prime hunting.

After supper the throng began to flow in our direction, and kept flowing, until our hilltop tent was like a ship in the middle of an ocean of caribou. At midnight, with the light all glowing and golden, my heart soared and about flew away. *Hey, Jonah, they're still here.* And so are you, looking over my shoulder. Hunter's paradise!

Caribou grazed their way up and onto our little hilltop. Cows lay down no more than twenty feet away to rest and chew their cud. One plopped down and took a nap at my feet. I started taking pictures. Ryan had been taking hundreds all this while. "You and I are in the middle of the Serengeti of North America," Ryan said.

Of the pictures I snapped myself, I felt the best about one I took around three in the morning. I took it from low on our hillside as three magnificent bulls were fording the river from right to left. I snapped it with the bulls in the right half of the picture and open water on the left. The background was filled with that ocean of caribou lapping against the bare mountains.

Around five in the morning we took pictures of a grizzly parting the caribou as it lumbered by the foot of our hill. A couple hours later, from a hundred yards, we watched a mother grizzly trying to wrestle down an old bull in the shallows of the river. Her two small cubs were all agitated at the sidelines. For a good long while the bull was able to fend her off with his antlers. Finally she put a move on him and got him by the neck, took him down, and finished him off. Ryan's motor drive was whirring all the while.

As it turned out, the mother grizzly and cubs never got a bite to eat. A boar grizzly ran the sow off. She couldn't defend her cubs and the carcass at the same time. The male opened up the carcass of the bull caribou, only to have a pack of seven wolves show up and harass him into giving it up.

Other than that, we didn't see any caribou fall prey to the wolves and bears. We couldn't see what was going on at the fringes of the enormous herd. All morning the clouds were thickening, and by noon, thunder was rumbling. We pulled on our rain shells and rain pants. A sheet of dark rain fell like a curtain in front of the peak at the head of the valley. A lightning bolt struck the peak, and thunder came rumbling toward us. Caribou by the thousands—who'd been lying down, chewing their cud—rose to their feet in alarm.

A couple minutes later a second bolt of lightning broke loose with a searing crack, like the sky was breaking open. The thunder that came with it was like an atomic explosion. The whole valley shook; my teeth rattled. The caribou stampeded every which way, terrified out of their skulls.

I was terrified out of mine. I'd never been in a thunderstorm, only seen some from a distance, not very many. I turned to Ryan, who was calmly photographing the nearest caribou as they stampeded off our hilltop.

"What do we do?" I cried.

"What *can* we do?" he replied with a crazy grin. "Look at 'em go! It's like a tidal wave!"

"Your hair is standing on end!"

"So is yours!"

The next bolt came in like a missile. I thought I was dead. The explosion of thunder about knocked my head off.

Amazingly, we were alive and intact. There was a strange, sharp smell in the air. My brother was still shooting pictures of those masses of caribou running like the wind. The next bolt of lightning struck three of them dead no more than a hundred yards away.

The rain began to fall like bullets. Ryan stuffed his camera inside of his camera bag, which he pressed to his belly underneath his rain shell.

"Should we get in the tent?"

"Let's get off this hilltop, and fast!"

We hustled down to the river bottom and huddled on the tundra, water pooling all around us. If the next bolt had our name on it, I was going to beat Jonah to the hereafter.

Ryan had his hood pulled tight around his face. His beard was streaming water like he was standing under a showerhead. He was pumped up and giddy. "Ever seen a storm like this, Nick?"

"Never!" Another bolt broke loose. "Hope we live through it!"

"Weird weather for the Arctic!"

"Tell me about it!"

By now there wasn't a caribou to be seen. The rain continued but the lightning had moved on, down the valley to the north. Ryan said it was okay to go back up to the tent. Once inside, I asked my brother if they have thunderstorms like that in Arizona. "Every summer," he said.

"Jonah doesn't like it one bit. Lightning storms aren't right up here. Not natural."

"Your summers used to be too cool for big thunderstorms to get going."

"We hear it's because we've lost our summer ice in the Beaufort Sea, but I don't get the connection."

"I'll give it a try. All that dark open water absorbs heat and gives off way more evaporation than you got off the ice. Moist air and heat are prime ingredients for thunderstorms. The sea and the land both are warmer than they used to be."

"You can keep the heat down south, far as I'm concerned!"

With that we quit jawing and struck the tent. Before long we were hoisting our packs and pointing our feet west toward the Firth River. We'd got what we'd come for, and I was homeward bound.

20

TURNING FOR HOME

Climbing out of the valley, Ryan had a satisfied smile on his face, and so did I. We had witnessed something few will ever see. The struggle we had gone through to get there made the winning of it all the sweeter.

At the top of the pass, we rested with our packs off. I had always held so much of myself back, but not anymore. I told Ryan he should come back with me to Aklavik and take pictures for his article. "I'd love to," my brother said.

"From Aklavik, we'll boat out to Shingle Point. You can stay with us in our cabin. Half of Aklavik will be out there fishing for char and whitefish, and trying to fill our quota of beluga whales. You should ask the old hunters about the sea ice, how much of it used to last through the summer. Ask about the winds—seems like every summer there's fewer days we can get out on the ocean. Ask about the storms that are chewing up the coast and even drowning polar bears. The hunters are the ones to talk to."

"Thanks—my article would be so much better with their input. And yes, I'd love to go on from Aklavik to Shingle Point. We're only getting started. You're like an iceberg, Nick. There's a lot more than meets the eye."

"Same as you. You haven't told me anything about your family."

"Well, I've got a brother in Aklavik. . . ."

I gave him a poke. "Who else is there?"

"You're it. I was an only, and my mother passed away a few years ago. Her marriage to our father didn't last long. They were divorced when I was just a little guy, four or so. He came to see me a few times, but I never really had a chance to get to know him."

We hoisted our packs and started down the other side of the pass. On the flats below, we walked side by side. Ryan said, "Nick, have you ever heard the theory that climate change might be a factor in the decline of caribou herds in the Arctic?"

"Lots of times. From Jonah."

"What's his explanation?"

"Warmer weather. We're having freezing rain sometimes in September and October when it should be snowing. Sometimes it even happens in November and December. Where our caribou spend the winter—mostly south of the Porcupine River—the people at Old Crow say the same thing is happening. The caribou have to be able to dig through the snow to get at the lichens to make it through the winter. Caribou hooves and antlers are made for digging through snow, but there's no way they can get at the feed when it's under a thick sheet of ice."

Ryan had been hanging on every word. "Get this, Nick. What you told me is exactly what the scientists are recently beginning to report. That's what might have caused the huge die-off in the Bathurst herd."

"Like Jonah always says, they should just ask us. But what does it mean about the future of the caribou?"

"One thing's for sure. If we mess with their calving grounds, they're finished."

"Say that in your article, okay?"

"It'll be in quotes, from caribou experts like Ken. Here's something else that will be in there: scientists questioning the wisdom of going after oil in the Arctic, whether it's under the calving grounds of the caribou or the floor of the Beaufort Sea. The Arctic is a high-risk environment. Does it make any sense to go after fossil fuels up here when burning them will only warm the earth even more? We should be developing renewable energy instead."

"We've got a teacher at school—Ross Archie, a fellow Inuk—who says the same thing. Ross told us about an Inuit leader who sued the United States for burning too much oil and coal. She says we have the right to be cold."

"That's a good one. What would people in Aklavik think if the Beaufort Sea became like the Gulf of Mexico, full of offshore oil platforms?"

"Depends on who you talk to. It would bring jobs and better houses and things to buy, but it might hurt the fishing and the sealing and the whaling. Jonah told me once that as long as we get our own food from the land and the ocean, we'll still be the Real People. Nobody at Aklavik wants to lose that, even if we have to spend time away working in the mines or whatever."

"Or the offshore oil rigs, if and when they get built?"

"You have to make money somehow to buy gas for your motorboat and snowmobile so you can keep fishing and trapping and hunting. Gas is way expensive up here."

My brother looked like this wasn't what he was hoping to hear, but what could I say? We shouldered our packs and started out again. By six in the evening the clouds were back, and they were growing dark. Ryan tried to raise Whitehorse on the satellite phone without any luck. The clouds or the peaks were blocking the signal. Both of us were eager to hear what that storm system was up to, the one Ken Logan was concerned about.

Two hours later we were all worn out. No wonder, after our all-nighter with the caribou. We pitched the tent by a small stream on the tundra. Dwarf fireweed was in bloom along the shore. We heated up some soup on the backpacking stove and added noodles. While it was cooking, we ate cheese and crackers and salami. The sun was out again, so we weren't as worried about the weather. After supper Ryan gave Whitehorse another try, hoping to catch Ken before he went to bed.

This time the call went through. "Heads up," Ken said. "That big low-pressure system off Alaska has finally quit spinning like a top and sucking up energy. It's on the move, guys. Most of the computer models have it meeting up with a big Arctic system brewing in the Beaufort Sea. Looks like those two systems are going to collide over the north slope of the Yukon Territory."

"Uh-oh," Ryan said. "Nick and I are in the cross-hairs. When is this smash-up supposed to happen?"

"Couple-three days."

"Ouch. Maybe we can get out in a hurry."

"Ask him about the grolar bear," I said. "Where is it right now?"

Ryan gave me a look like I was borrowing trouble.

"If it's anywhere near us," I insisted, "we need to know."

"I hear you, Nick," the biologist said. "It'll take just a minute. Hang on, guys."

When Ken Logan came back on, he said, "Here's your update. The grolar bear is still moving west along the coast. At present it's nearing Kay Point, maybe thirty miles east of the mouth of the Firth."

This time Ryan gave me a look that acknowledged I was right to be worried. There was something else in it, too—eagerness, maybe even excitement. "Thanks—we'll keep an eye out. Leave me a message if that bear reaches the Firth."

"Maybe you'll get a photo, is that what you're thinking?"

"I wouldn't mind, from a safe distance."

"Take care, you guys."

The two of them signed off. I said to my brother, "You still don't get it."

"What can I say? I'm a wildlife photographer."

"I still say they should've killed it."

"If it's a creature of climate change, there'll be more of them."

"Maybe so, but if they're anything like this one, look out."

I glanced at our pitched tent. "Hey, Ryan, maybe I'm not as tired as I thought. Let's get out of here. The sooner we fly out, the better. How much river do we have left to run?"

"It's right around thirty miles to Nunaluk Spit, where Red's going to pick us up."

"Could we get there tomorrow?"

"Sure don't think so. We have too much ground to cover to reach the Firth, and we have to put the raft back together."

"If we hike like maniacs, then stay on the water around the clock, how soon could we get to the finish line and fly out?"

Ryan closed his eyes and thought about it. "Noon, the day after tomorrow, barring unforeseen complications."

"Call Red. If we're talking about him picking us up at noon the day after tomorrow, now is not too soon."

"You're right. I hope I can reach him."

The old bush pilot picked up. What a relief to hear his

coarse-as-gravel Texas accent. "Howdy, Ryan. You get what you were after?"

"Sure did, Red, and then some."

"And now you got hot showers on the brain. How soon you talking about?"

"Day after tomorrow. Noon if that's good with you."

"You'll recall I cautioned you that flying out is subject to weather delay."

"We remember."

"Well, we're looking at major wind tomorrow afternoon, and I've got another party to fetch the next morning, weather permitting. That couple showed up, the ones from Montana I was telling you about. They started down the Firth nine days after you. Seen 'em?"

"Not yet."

"You will, on the last stretch of river or else camping at the spit. I'll try to get you out right after I do them, weather permitting. We'll see how it goes. We might be in for a major storm. I would recommend another pilot, but right now I'm the only game in town."

"Appreciate it, Red. We'll be looking for you the day after tomorrow."

"Weather permitting. You boys call me tomorrow evening. I'll give you the update."

Ryan signed off. We packed up and hit the ground

running. Within a few minutes I realized I could have asked about Jonah. Red probably knew if Jonah was still hanging on.

Midnight arrived without a breath of wind. A storm might be on the way, but the only clouds in sight were the clouds of bugs illuminated by the flat amber light. We were moving fast, with the humidity much higher than normal. "We're sweating like pigs!" Ryan exclaimed.

"Never seen a pig," I said, "but I'll take your word for it."

The dead calm lasted clear through the morning. It was still holding at noon, when we finally caught sight of the Firth from the ridge above Canyon Creek. By chance, we spied a yellow raft on the river. Had we reached that spot a minute later, we wouldn't have seen it at all. There were two people in it, a boatman on the oars and a passenger up front.

"Must be that couple from Montana," Ryan said. "No wonder they're in a hurry . . . they're planning on camping on the spit this evening."

Just then the yellow raft disappeared in the canyon. We were eager to rig ours and float as far as we could before the big wind arrived. We hustled down from the ridge.

Thirty minutes later we reached our rolled-up raft and the rest of the gear. We'd no sooner got there than the wind arrived with a roar. It went from flat calm to a gale in less than a minute.

This wasn't a gust or two. The wind was blowing full bore. "Wait it out?" I wondered aloud.

Ryan rubbed his beard against the grain. "I'm afraid we shouldn't. If a major storm is on the heels of the wind, the river is going to flood so bad it would be unrunnable. Grab the river guide, would you?"

Ryan leafed to the maps and found the ones for the lower canyon and the delta. "There's five camping spots in the last fourteen miles of the canyon, but I wouldn't trust any of them not to flood. Look, here's a campsite beyond the canyon, on the east side just two miles into the delta—Last Mountain Camp. That's got to be a safer bet than camping in the canyon if the river floods. With multiple channels running across the coastal plain, the floodwater will spread out."

We set to work. First thing, we carried the rolled-up raft down to a sandy spot at the mouth of Canyon Creek, only yards away from the Firth's powerful current. We hustled back for the foot pump and enough rope to tie the raft in four directions while Ryan was pumping it up. On my way back for more gear, the wind nearly blew me over. I remembered we hadn't called Whitehorse that morning or checked for messages. Now's not the time, I thought.

I kept shuttling gear to the raft. It took us another hour to assemble the oar frame, load the gear, and strap everything down. At last we were ready. I stood behind the raft, ready to give the boat a push when Ryan gave the word. He took one last look at the guidebook, checking what it said about the rapids ahead. After stowing the book, he looked over his shoulder to see if I was ready. I gave him a nervous nod. "Let's do it!" Ryan yelled into the wind.

I gave the raft a push and kept low as I moved forward along the side of the raft. I took my seat on the front cross tube and hung on tight. Before we escaped the canyon, we had twenty-three rapids to run.

21

THE BEAR AT LAST MOUNTAIN

Ryan pushed a couple strokes on the oars, out onto the river. The current took us like we had hooked on to a high-speed cable. Ryan pivoted the boat and rowed to the center of the river. Once there, he straightened the raft out so I was looking directly downstream over the front. In seconds we were going to drop into the first rapid.

I took a look over my shoulder. My brother was grinning from ear to ear. "There is nothing, absolutely nothing," he cried, "like messing around in boats!"

The canyon was at its deepest in those last fourteen miles. The walls bristled with thin layers of rock thrust up into the air, their edges sharp as swords. Clouds were gathering in a frightening hurry. We lost the sun. The gusts were so intense, the raft was getting blown this way and that, making the rapids all the more difficult. Ryan made the adjustments and ran the gauntlet.

It was something. *Exciting* and *thrilling* and *chilling* don't begin to describe the crashing white water in those fourteen miles. *Heart-stopping* comes closer. In the howling wind, it was totally insane. *In your face!*

By my watch, that run took an hour and fifty minutes. It felt like a whole lot less.

With the canyon at an end and the last rapid at our backs, I turned around and gave a cheer. "How'd you do that, Ryan?"

"With difficulty!" Still breathing hard, he put the oar handles under his knees and leaned forward to meet my fist bump.

We floated out of the mountains and onto the coastal plain. As the Firth flowed onto land that was all but flat, the river split into two channels, one on either side of an island of gravel.

At the speed the thunderstorm was moving, it would soon be upon us. We pulled on our rain gear.

The lightning and thunder drew closer. The wind out of the south was sweeping the water off the river and throwing it in our faces. A couple miles ahead, a huge hill with a spiny crest rose all on its lonesome out of the left bank of the river, one last vestige of the foothills on the flat coastal plain. The hill had a name: Last Mountain.

I was eager to get off the river, pitch our tent, and crawl inside. "We still gonna camp at the Last Mountain campsite, Ryan?"

"I'm planning on it, even if that couple from Montana is there. At a time like this, I bet they'd be thrilled to have the company. The map shows the campsite at the mouth of the creek just upstream of the mountain. Keep an eye out, so we don't slide by."

I could see from the map that the Firth ran in braids through the delta, a maze of river channels among gravel islands. Just ahead, two islands rose from the river, separating the flow into three channels. Ryan pushed on the oars and steered us into the channel farthest left, where we needed to be. I reached for the binoculars and glassed the shore upstream from the foot of Last Mountain. I saw a splash of gold there, in front of the man-high willows that grew along the creek. "Think I see a tent, Ryan."

Our new channel was thigh deep, without a strong current. On the coastal plain, the Firth had lost its punch. I got a good look at the campsite through the binoculars. "Yep, it's a tent, but it's flat on the ground. Wind must've collapsed it. Camp table got blown over too. Lots of gulls down there."

"Where's the couple's raft?"

"I can see it through the willows. It's parked in the mouth of the creek—that yellow raft we saw running the canyon."

"See him or her?"

"Sure don't. Maybe they had a bear in camp."

"Why do you say that?"

"The gulls wouldn't hang around unless they found something to scavenge."

"Maybe those folks left some food out," Ryan said. "Maybe they're climbing the mountain."

"In this weather? I don't like the looks of this. Let's not land there, okay?"

"You got it. We'll land on the island across from the camp. See if we can figure anything out."

"You don't have to land on the island, Ryan. You can hover in the slow water close to its shore, and watch from the boat."

"How come you don't want to land?"

"This channel's getting shallower. A bear could charge across it like nothing. We wouldn't have time to get away if we leave the boat and have to get back in."

"You really think there's a bear over there, don't you?"

"There might be. Can't tell, with all the willow brush."

Ryan kept us well away from the camp as he let the

current take us downstream. The wind was blowing gale force, and it looked like the racing clouds were going to drop a deluge any minute. Ryan pulled into six inches of water alongside the shore of the island opposite the campsite. He shipped his oars. I glassed across seventy-five yards of water to the collapsed tent in a small clearing among clumps of willows. Ryan got out his big black Nikon with the long lens and began to take pictures of the disorder at the Last Mountain campsite.

The cries of the gulls still had me spooked. I felt for the bear protection at my side. My bear banger pouch was still there, and the launcher was loaded. Ryan had our only can of pepper spray holstered to his belt. How I wanted my rifle in my hands. I thought I saw some movement behind a gap in the blowing willows. Just then a bolt of lightning struck Last Mountain. I flinched, and the binoculars jumped.

I tried again. This time, through the willows, I spotted the head and the motions of a feeding bear. A grizzly, I thought—the head and the forelimbs were shades of brown. The grizzly had something pinned to the ground, and was ripping meat from it. Something about the claws wasn't right. They weren't as long as a grizzly's. "Bear in camp," I whispered. "Behind the willows."

"Where behind the willows?"

"To the right of the tent and behind it—sight on the gap between the two big clumps of willows."

I looked again and got a better view as the bear stopped feeding and peered directly through the small break in the willow brush. Now I could see its body. The bulk of it was covered with dirty white fur. "It's the grolar bear, Ryan."

"You're pulling my leg."

"I wish I was. Look, he's got a satellite collar around his neck."

Ryan adjusted his lens. "Now I see him." He took three quick pictures. "Come out in the open, big fella. Let's get a look at you."

At that moment, the bear lumbered through the brush and into a clearing. Its strange patchwork coat was on full display. Ryan's shutter whirred and whirred. "How bizarre is that," he said under his breath. "Just like you said—more like a grizzly's head, more like a polar bear's body, except for the brown legs. Whoa, he's huge."

I held my breath, hoping the grolar bear wasn't on to us. So far it wasn't.

The grolar bear went to feed on something behind the tussock grass. Next time it lifted its head, it had a human arm, elbow to fingers, in its jaws.

"Oh no," I said. "Oh no."

"Get the sat phone," Ryan said under his breath.

"Make the call before the storm breaks. We might lose the signal."

"Who do I call?"

"The numbers are on the inside lid of the ammo can. Start with Search and Rescue in Inuvik. They'll dispatch a helicopter."

I tried to unbuckle the lid as silently as possible, but it opened with a screech. I looked across the river. The grolar bear rose to its full height, with that arm still in its mouth. Ryan took a picture. I stopped breathing. We held dead still.

I couldn't be sure the beast was on to us. The grolar bear dropped the arm, then walked in our direction, three upright steps to the shore. Ryan took another picture. The bear woofed at us two, three times, then came down on all fours, growled, and laid back its ears—Ryan taking pictures all the while. "Ryan," I whispered. "Let's slip out of here before it decides to charge."

"You got it!"

The bear woofed again.

Ryan didn't take the time to put away the camera. He let it hang from his neck as he reached for the oars. I snapped the lid of the ammo can closed so our sat phone couldn't get wet. I'd have to wait to make the call; rain was sweeping toward us in sheets from the mountains. Ryan began to ply the oars. Soon as he did, the grolar bear charged into the river.

Lightning struck barely downstream, shocking me half to death. Unfazed, the bear kept charging. By the time Ryan reached the current, and had the raft moving as fast as he could possibly power it, the bear was closing on us fast, splashing through the river with unbelievable speed. Ryan stopped rowing, but why?

When I turned around and looked, he was handing me the pepper spray out of its holster. "Here, take it," he cried. I did, and he started rowing again.

By chance, we were over deeper water. Soon, the bear was too. Rather than swim after us, the grolar bear swam toward the shallows bordering the island. It hauled out on the island and started racing after us along the shore. "Good grief," Ryan said, "the thing is a monster, like you said."

Ryan was heaving on the oars with all his might. Pulling the raft downstream meant looking over his shoulder to see where he was going. Somehow he was able to keep in the fastest current. I was looking upstream off the front of the boat. My eyes were on the bear as it raced down the shore of the island. It was about to draw even with us where the island came to an end.

As the current swept us around the bottom of the island toward the current coming in from the other side, the grolar bear plunged into the river with a roar.

The thing swam faster than I would have thought possible. It was gaining on us, breath whooshing in and out of its nostrils. The beast was twenty feet behind us and closing.

I looked back at Ryan, my eyes begging for more speed. "Boat's heavy," he panted. "Get ready with the pepper spray. Safety off?"

"Safety off!"

"In this wind, you'll have to wait until it's close!"

"How close?"

"So much wind . . . arm's length!"

When I looked, the bear's face was right there, no more than ten feet away from me. The grolar bear's small amber eyes were filled with the same rage I'd seen on the Mackenzie. With powerful strokes, the creature quickly closed the gap. Up came a paw, about to slash the raft. I leaned forward and blasted the monster's face. Its flailing claws knocked the pepper spray into the river.

I could barely see, I could barely breathe.

"You got him!" Ryan cried.

My eyes and my throat were on fire. "I got myself!"

"The bear got the worst of it! He's heading for shore— can't even swim straight."

"Glad to hear it," I managed.

Ten minutes later the searing pain was backing off, and I could function again. We were onshore, in a torrent of rain. Ryan had the sat phone out, and was punching numbers without even trying to protect it from the rain. He reached Search and Rescue in Inuvik and told them what we had seen at Last Mountain campsite. The dispatcher asked if one or both of the victims might be alive. Ryan said he didn't think so but didn't know for sure. "How soon can you come?" he asked.

"No time soon, if the forecast is right. Maybe not for three days. Has the storm arrived at the delta of the Firth River?"

"Big-time."

"It might turn into what they're calling 'a marine bomb.' Shingle Point has been evacuated. Hang on—we can't fly in this weather. We'll get to you as soon as we can."

That was the last we heard. A bolt of lightning downstream sent a herd of musk oxen stampeding by us, heading upriver. The blast was like that bomb they were talking about. The thunder kept rolling, right through my bones. "Signal's gone," Ryan reported.

22

IN THE TEETH OF THE STORM

The rain was falling harder and faster than I'd ever seen, and the winds were ferocious. Ryan stowed the sat phone. "You hear what the man said, Nick?"

"Help is not on the way."

"Is your family out at Shingle Point?" The rain was so loud, Ryan was practically shouting.

"I sure don't think so. Some people go in late June, but we always wait for July. This time, there's no way they would go early."

"You don't have to worry about your family, but they've heard about this storm and must be worried about you. You want to try to call them right now?"

"The signal's out, and we'd ruin the phone in the rain.

We don't have time to mess around! We can't row back upstream. . . . The river's going to flood, isn't it?"

"It's gonna flood something awful, and soon. I can't picture a safe place to camp on the delta—the whole thing is a floodplain."

"So what can we do?"

"I think we have to run the rest of the river through the delta and hole up on Nunaluk Spit. Have you ever been there?"

"About five years ago, with Jonah. It was a really long way from Shingle Point."

"How high above sea level is it?"

"I don't know; maybe ten, fifteen feet?"

"That's not very much. How big are your tides up here?"

"They don't amount to much—a couple of feet."

"What does the spit look like?"

"It's an island made out of gravel and stones. I remember seeing windbreaks—quite a few—made out of driftwood. The people who raft the Firth build them while they're waiting for an airplane."

Ryan went for his spiral-bound guidebook and turned to the maps for the delta and the shore of the Beaufort Sea. The waterproof pages were getting the supreme test. The rain was coming so heavy that I could have collected a cup of water off my brother's beard in half a minute. "It's not going to be pretty out on the coast," Ryan said, "but what other choice do we have?"

"You're right, we have to go for the coast and hope for the best."

"At least we've got the boat to jump into if the sea washes over the spit."

Ryan showed me the map of the Firth running across its delta. In its last fourteen miles the Firth split into dozens and dozens of channels. My job, every time Ryan had to make a choice, was to point his way into the one carrying the most water. Make a wrong call and we would get stuck in a channel to nowhere. In the wind and the rain, with the world gone dark under heavy clouds and my eyes seared from the pepper spray, I had to find the way.

We shoved off. Almost immediately, the channel we were on branched into three. I pointed Ryan down the one on the right. This was crazy. The split-second decisions had my heart pounding. Somehow I kept making good calls. In the delta's last mile, Ryan had to row hard to keep us off a wall of ice ten or twelve feet high. Finally, the channel we were following flowed into the saltwater lagoon between the mainland and Nunaluk Spit.

Half a mile of white-capped open water lay between us and the spit. In the storm, we couldn't see that far. We wouldn't have had a prayer of making the crossing if the wind wasn't blowing north toward the spit. While the wind was with us, we had to give it a try even though the lagoon was whipped into a frenzy.

The crossing was more than ugly. Waves kept crashing over the side, a mixture of freezing sea and river water. At last the spit came into view through a heavy curtain of rain. I jumped ashore with the rope and held the raft. Ryan came off the boat, green eyes blazing. "Let's haul it out of the water, Nick, beach it as far up as we can!"

On the count of three, we jerked the raft maybe four feet onto the gravel. My brother got in my face and yelled, "You stay with the boat! I'm gonna go find one of those windbreaks for us!"

"Got it!" I yelled as a gust of wind nearly blew me off my feet. I had to brace against the raft to keep from going down.

Within seconds, Ryan disappeared in the rain and the wind and the eerie near-darkness. Evenings were normally bright as can be at the end of June, but the storm was blotting out the sun.

After about fifteen minutes alone, I wished I had told my brother not to be picky. He might get lost, or blown off the spit into the Beaufort.

Ryan materialized out of the storm a few minutes later. "Found a five-star hotel!" he hollered.

That turned out to be a five-star exaggeration. The windbreak was chest high and three-sided, made of driftwood. The whole coast is strewn with the stuff. It comes all the way down the Mackenzie from where the big trees grow.

For the time being, our windbreak was no windbreak at all. It had been built for protection against the wind off the ocean, not the mountains. It was a battle to get the tent up and secure its rain fly. We used all twenty-seven stakes and tied the corners off to heavy logs.

The spit was a couple miles long and generally about a hundred yards wide. Jonah and I had landed the motorboat here when I was ten, and had lunch behind one of the windbreaks. An hour before, we'd been on Herschel Island, where we visited the historical park with the buildings from the old whaling station. Some of the graves in the Native cemetery on Herschel had recently washed away during a storm.

Here I was in a storm worse than that one. It might even be worse than the one when I was six. Back then the coastal community of Tuktoyaktuk lost big chunks of the land that protected it from the sea.

Ryan's tent was taking a terrible beating. The storm

raged on, and the wind—still out of the south—was horrendous. We lay in our sleeping bags and talked about the flood coming down the Firth River, what that must be like. We could hear the roar coming from the back of the lagoon where the river met the sea. "The canyon must be brimful," I said. Ryan said he believed I was right.

"Do you think one or the other of the couple from Montana might still be alive, Nick?"

"I saw the bear feeding in two different places. Sure don't think so."

Ryan had brought his precious camera box off the raft, and had it with him in the tent. He showed me the pictures of the grolar bear he had taken from the raft. The one of the bear standing up with the arm in its jaws made my blood curdle. "Will that be in *National Geographic*?"

"I'm glad you asked me that," Ryan said. "There. I just deleted it."

"Why'd you do that?"

"It would go viral. People would get the wrong idea. I would never want to demonize bears."

"But that one *is* a demon."

"I know, but maybe the grolar bears to come won't be like this one. I'll write about what this one did, and call it a man-eater, but I'll also say that the grolar bear appears to be a creature of climate change, and climate change is the beast we should be worrying about. I've even heard it put that way, by a scientist who'd been studying the increase in severe storms around the world the last ten, fifteen years."

"What did he say?"

"That the climate has become a beast, and we are poking it with sticks."

I thought about what Jonah had said about everything changing, and all the bad signs. *We're going to have to deal with whatever comes*, Jonah had said. *We just have to adapt.*

I put my head down and gave in to my exhaustion. The sleep I got was anything but restful. That last thing Ryan had said—about poking a beast with sticks—worked its way into my fears. I dreamed I was trying to fend off the grolar bear with a chunk of driftwood.

I woke up hours later, with a start, to lightning and thunder. Wind was buffeting the tent so bad, Ryan was bracing the poles with his outstretched arms.

"This is unreal," I said.

"The wind's coming from both directions now, north as well as south."

"Those two storms are colliding, like Ken said?"

"Yep, the storm off the Beaufort is on us now, too."

Before long, the wind blew only from the north. The storm off the ocean was more powerful than the one that had crossed Alaska. The rain wasn't so loud on the tent anymore. I peeked outside and found out why. The rain had turned to wet snow, blowing horizontal off the sea.

"Don't worry," Ryan said. "We're in the best four-season tent money can buy."

Suddenly I realized that the sound of the surf on the ocean side of the spit was much louder than before. "Hear those waves crashing, Ryan?"

Ryan reached for his rain gear. "Sounds bad. I'm going out for a look."

My brother was gone for about ten minutes. Before he came back inside, he shook the snow off the tent fly. He didn't say anything as he crawled through the vestibule, shucking his rain gear along the way.

"What's up, Ryan?"

"The waves are. The Beaufort Sea is surging against the spit. Let's hope the wind doesn't get worse, or we'll be swimming."

After he said that, there was no going back to sleep. Time slowed down. I kept checking my watch, and that didn't help a bit. Ryan looked grim. Twenty minutes later—half past three in the morning—I said, "Is it getting worse, or is it my imagination?"

Big brother pulled on his beard. "It's not your imagi-nation. I'll take another look."

"I'll do it this time."

"You stay put."

"No, I want to see for myself."

"Okay, we'll both go."

We pulled on our rain gear, crawled out of the tent, and staggered into the teeth of the storm. By this time of day we should have had no end of light to see by, but the clouds were too thick. We had to lean forward into the wind and snow to keep from being blown over. The crashing of the surf boomed louder as we got closer, and the salt spray stung our faces.

Closer yet, enormous white waves appeared in the murk. The wind-driven seas were up like I couldn't believe. A towering breaker was about to crash on the shore. It was awful to look at, by far the biggest surf I'd ever laid eyes on.

That wave broke across the top of the spit. We turned tail and ran hard to get out of its reach. Looking east down the spit, I saw the same wave race clear across it. When the surf hit a big windbreak, it broke those timbers down like they were matchsticks.

Luckily, our tent was on higher ground, but not by

much. We had a few minutes, and we needed them to stuff our sleeping bags and strike the tent. With our river bags over our shoulders, we hustled toward the raft. I looked back and saw a wave demolish the windbreak that had sheltered our tent.

The storm surge swept over that whole stretch of the spit as Ryan rowed us into the lagoon.

23

TOO HUGE, TOO POWERFUL

Ryan had to heave on the oars to keep from being blown across the lagoon and onto the mainland shore, where the flooding Firth was dumping into salt-water. We heard the river but couldn't see it. We couldn't see more than a hundred yards.

Where to now? The wind was howling, and the storm showed no sign of letting up. The snow was coming hard as ever, wind-whipped and salty.

"We need someplace to go," Ryan said. "You were here once before, Nick. Any ideas?"

"I was on the ocean side of the spit, not in the lagoon."

Ryan gritted his teeth and kept rowing. All kinds of

driftwood had swept over the spit, and he had to work hard to avoid it.

I said, "What if we just let the wind take us to the shore? Maybe we can find a place where the Firth isn't flooding."

"We might get pinned by the driftwood, and not be able to get back on the lagoon. If the tubes get punctured, we're sunk."

There had to be an answer. Rowing with all his might, Ryan was losing ground against the wind. I couldn't see the mainland shore yet, but the lagoon was only half a mile wide. We would be there soon, willing or not.

I racked my brain, trying to remember what I had seen when I was with Jonah. Like I told Ryan, we'd been on the ocean side of the spit.

Even so, had I seen anything that might help?

I closed my eyes and tried to bring it back. I remembered the blue sky, the calm seas, and us heading farther west along Nunaluk Spit. Jonah had pointed out something for me to look at.

What was it?

Now I remembered: a cabin, close to the end of the spit, that was named after a white explorer. Jonah motored closer so I could get a better look. The cabin was made of driftwood logs, ax-hewn and squared into timbers. The rise it was perched on didn't look raw and stony like the rest of the spit. It was carpeted with tundra. The greenery, now that I thought of it, explained why the cabin was still standing after a hundred years. It was built on ground high enough above sea level to be out of reach of even the worst storm waves.

"Stefansson's cabin!" I shouted, like I'd been underwater and was coming up for air.

"Who's Stefansson?"

"An explorer!"

"But where is it?"

"Near the west end of the spit! It's on high ground! Row west!"

"Got it!" Ryan cried as he pivoted the raft. With his eye on the breakers washing over the spit, he began to quarter against the wind and snow. After twenty minutes of hard labor Ryan sang out, "Has it got a roof on it?"

"Yep," I shouted into the wind, "with a stovepipe sticking out!"

"Dry firewood stacked by the stove?"

"We didn't land there, just passed by."

"Stefansson's B and B, here we come! Tell me more about this guy!"

"I have no idea what he was exploring. Bet he didn't discover anything we didn't already know about!"

Our B and B was only a mile down the spit from where

we had pitched our tent. That was the most difficult mile I ever hope to travel. We had more than the wind and the snow to contend with. Surging over the spit, the angry sea kept throwing driftwood in our path. I fended it off with a long stick as Ryan gave his all on the oars.

At last the cabin appeared through falling snow and tossing waves. It was perched on a knoll with a swath of green around it like I remembered. The knoll didn't look as high as before, but that was because the sea was up. For the time being, the cabin was out of reach of the waves.

What a relief it was to get off the water. The cabin's heavy, bear-proof door was latched but unlocked. We stepped inside, closed the door, and stood there shedding the weather on the floorboards. My eyes went to the dry firewood off to one side of the stove. My brother and I shared a smile.

We leaned our river bags against the wall. The furnishings and decoration didn't add up to much: a simple table and chairs, a guest book to sign, and an old whaling harpoon on the wall. I remembered Jonah saying that the cabin had been restored by the historical park on Herschel Island.

With the snow turning to sleet, we looked seaward out the four-paned window and saw fearsome waves pounding the shore less than thirty yards away. "This cabin sat much farther back from the sea five years ago," I said.

Ryan looked grim. "The Beaufort Sea must be rearranging the whole coast right now. Chewing it up and spitting it out. We can only hope this isn't the storm that brings this cabin down."

We holed up there through heavy winds and rain all through that day and into the next. We kept trying the sat phone as the storm raged on but couldn't raise a signal. The problem might have been the dousing it took during that emergency call in the pouring rain.

At last the storm gave out. The sky was clearing. Out the open front door, to the east, the broad back of Herschel Island was taking shape out of the dissolving fog. Stefansson's cabin didn't have much of a future. On the ocean side, most of the knoll was gone. Fewer than ten yards remained between the cabin and a twenty-foot drop to the Beaufort Sea.

We finally got a signal on the sat phone. The first number Ryan tried was Red Wiley's. We were hoping he could come and get us that day.

Our bush pilot was hugely relieved to hear from us. In all his years in the North, he'd never seen a storm this bad. Red said that Search and Rescue was guessing we had continued on to Nunaluk Spit after calling from the Firth's delta to report the grolar bear attack. They wondered if we were holed up in Stefansson's cabin, but they weren't sure the cabin would survive the record levels of storm surge on the coast. "Jonah said Nick would remember about the cabin," Red told Ryan.

My heart leaped. "Jonah's alive!" I cried.

"Yes indeed, Nick, and he'll be awful happy to hear that you are, too."

"What about Shingle Point?"

"Everybody out there got evacuated. As for the cabins, heavy damage is likely." Red said he would try to get to us later in the day, but didn't know for sure if he would be able to land. It depended on how bad the storm had rearranged the spit. "It would be helpful if you boys hike the length of the spit and call me back with your report. I need a fairly level stretch with no driftwood and no rocks that have 'troublemaker' written on them. Snow on the ground?"

"Rain melted it," Ryan said.

"If you hear a chopper in the vicinity, that will be Search and Rescue. They left Inuvik an hour ago headed for the Firth River delta. They're on their way to the Last Mountain campsite on the Firth. The chopper pilot's got three officials aboard: an RCMP officer, a park warden, and a paramedic. I don't know if they'll give you a flyby—just thought you should know."

"If we find you a landing strip on the spit," Ryan said,

"we'll mark the center of it with a blue X. We've got a tarp we can cut up."

"Much obliged."

Red signed off. We ate breakfast and got ready for our hike. "Let's bring along all the bear protection we got," I said. "We're on the outer coast. There might be a polar bear scavenging for carcasses."

I had my hunting knife on one hip and bear banger pouch with loaded launcher on the other. Ryan had the air horn. I wished I hadn't lost our last can of pepper spray to the grolar bear.

My brother looked haggard. "Ready to go, Nick?"

"Almost," I said, and took the harpoon down from the wall. It might've been a hundred years old but appeared to be in good condition with no rust. The double-fluke head looked deadly, and where the steel shaft emerged from the wooden base, there wasn't a bit of wiggle. Maybe it was from late in the commercial whaling days and never got used. The great bowhead whales were so scarce at the last, the whalers couldn't find any. The ships sailed away and never came back.

We started east along the spit. It looked real different, new-made with sand and stones those awesome waves had tossed up. The surface had been scoured of driftwood; even the biggest logs were nowhere to be seen. We made the first tracks on the sloping beach. Halfway down the spit, we hadn't yet found a suitable landing strip.

From around a bend in the shore came the cries of gulls. That put me on guard. As we reached the bend we saw an awful sight: two polar bears washed up dead.

"Must've drowned in the storm," Ryan said. "A mother and yearling cub, maybe?"

Ryan started snapping pictures through his long lens. With the sun from the south, the light was good for photos. "Wait a second," he said. "I see a third bear, and it's moving. It's behind the bigger of the other two and chewing on it."

"Yeah, I see something."

"The third one isn't a polar bear, Nick."

"You sure?"

"It's got a brown head."

"I see it now. Must be a grizzly."

How wrong I was. Suddenly the bear stood up, tall as any polar bear. Only its head and legs were brown. The rest of its fur was dirty white.

My brother cursed under his breath.

"Of all the luck," I groaned.

Had the grolar bear seen us? I was afraid it had. It went to all fours, clambered over the polar bear it was feeding on, and stood again. We were in plain view, and the patchwork bear was looking directly at us. A wave of nausea ran through me.

"Oh, no," my brother muttered.

"Hold this harpoon," I told him. I opened the pouch on my hip and took out the launcher and a couple extra bangers. I made sure the launcher was loaded and switched the safety off. "Your air horn ready to go, Ryan?"

"All set." His voice was far from steady.

The grolar bear walked three steps before coming down to all fours. It woofed at us, then laid back its ears. It broke into a lope, running down the beach toward us but not at full speed.

Ryan said, "He just wants to see what we are. We can't turn our backs on him, I know that much."

In no time at all, the massive animal covered half the distance. I was about to shoot off a banger when the beast suddenly stopped and stood up for another look.

"Now!" Ryan cried, but I didn't need to be told. I raised the launcher, aimed above the bear, and fired. The weird whistling like an artillery shell hardly fazed it, and neither did the explosion like a gunshot above its head. I fired off a second and a third. Each time the creature flinched but didn't turn and run. The grolar bear came down onto all fours. It clacked its jaws, huffed once, woofed twice.

Then it charged, full-speed. I grabbed the harpoon

from Ryan's hands. "Air horn!" I yelled. Ryan set the thing off. Its trumpet let out a blast like the horn of an ice-road trucker.

The air horn stopped the monster in its tracks. The grolar bear hesitated, then opened its jaws wide and growled. I had the distinct feeling that the bear remembered us and wanted us dead. It showed no sign of backing off. "Give me the harpoon," Ryan barked. "I'll cover you. Run for the cabin!"

"No way. I wouldn't get that far. When he charges, give him the air horn again."

"You take it," Ryan said, and tried to hand me the air horn. I shook my head. Just then the bear charged. Ryan shoved the air horn at me and tore the harpoon from my hands. I got thrown off my feet.

Ryan took a few steps toward the oncoming bear. By the time I got off my knees, the grolar bear was nearly on him. As they met, Ryan lunged at the monster, trying to spear it. The beast was too huge, too powerful. With a slap of the bear's paw, the harpoon went flying.

Ryan went to the sand on his belly, hands behind his head. Growling in rage, the bear mauled him with bites to his back, hands, and skull. I scooped up the air horn and pulled the trigger. It had two more blasts in it, but the bear was unfazed. The monster fixed those awful eyes on me, then went back to mauling Ryan.

"Hey, freak!" I screamed as I ran for the harpoon. "Come and get me!"

I'd gotten the creature's attention. It turned away from my brother and took a couple steps toward me. The grolar bear stopped and roared, mouth full of bloody slobber.

"Come and get it," I screamed. "Yeah, you." I was trying to convince myself I could stand up to this thing.

I was going to have only one chance. I had to do this just right, exactly the way Jonah had told me, the way our ancestors had hunted polar bears for a thousand years and more. I once asked Jonah if it could be done in modern times. He said, "I don't see why not."

Here came my living nightmare, and my knees nearly buckled. The monster bounded close, then stood to its full height above me like it had on the banks of the Mackenzie, like I was hoping it would again. The bear raised its front legs high in the air, showing its claws and teeth, and roared.

I kept my weapon hidden the best I could, against my side. *You have to be patient*, I heard Jonah saying.

Down the beast came.

Eyes locked on its chest, right over the heart, I planted the butt of the harpoon in the sand and spread my hands along the weapon—one hand gripping steel, the other gripping wood—and held on tight. The angle was everything.

With all its power and fury, roaring horribly, the grolar bear came down on the tip of the harpoon, burying the barbed steel deep in its chest. But had I found the heart?

The beast stood to its full height once more, roaring with rage and disbelief and pain. Blood spouting from mouth and nostrils, the bear swiped at the harpoon but failed to dislodge it.

The grolar bear wouldn't go down. Now what?

The bear staggered forward, one paw poised to slash me open. I jumped back and drew my hunting knife.

I didn't have to use it. That freak of nature fell dead at my feet.

24

CHANGE COMES TO THE ARCTIC

Ryan got to his feet more concerned about his camera than himself. I think he was still in shock. I know I was. He started taking pictures of the dead bear. He asked me to kneel beside it. He took my picture. I looked solemn and grim.

People who've seen the article in *National Geographic* ask me what I was thinking right then. I tell them I have no idea. I was numb.

Soon as Ryan got his pictures, I pointed out that his hands were all bloody. So was his skull—he had some deep bite marks in it, and a flap of scalp was about to fall off the back of his head. I put the flap back in place and told him to keep his hand pressed down on it.

We hurried to the cabin. I ran for the first-aid box off the raft. I tended Ryan's wounds with cotton gauze and lots of disinfectant. My brother winced a few times but was tough as nails. He told me he had sutures and a needle and a needle puller in the first-aid box if I wanted to do stitches. I looked at him like he was crazy.

Ryan called Search and Rescue and told them he got mauled by the grolar bear. He described his injuries as not life threatening but said he was concerned about getting infected. Ryan asked if the helicopter at the Last Mountain campsite would come pick him up and fly him to the hospital in Inuvik.

"Sure thing. Your brother okay?"

"Unscathed."

"They're looking to shoot the grolar bear from the air. Is it still on the spit to your knowledge?"

"Without a doubt," Ryan said, and went on to explain why he was so sure.

A short while later we got a call from the park warden aboard the Search and Rescue helicopter—Dave Curry, from the Parks Canada office in Inuvik. He was calling from what had been the Last Mountain campsite. No trace of it remained. The flood that roared down the Firth River had rearranged its channels across the delta. The old islands were gone and new ones had been created. Last Mountain Camp was nothing but a rubble field, with no trace of the couple's bodies or gear. The chopper was headed our way.

When it arrived, as close to the cabin as it could land, Dave Curry said he'd just been in touch with Roger McKeon, who'd put the satellite collar on the grolar bear. McKeon had told him to keep watch over the bear's carcass. The helicopter was going to come back with a cargo net and fly the grolar bear to Inuvik, where it would be kept in cold storage until it could be scientifically examined.

I waved good-bye to my brother as the chopper took off. Ryan was taking pictures from up front, right out the bubble. The pilot flew low over the spit, and called Red Wiley with the news that he should be able to land on the eastern end of the island. I rowed the loaded raft through the lagoon down to the east end as the park warden, armed with a rifle, hiked down the beach to keep the grolar bear company. He hoped to keep the birds away from its eyes.

That evening I called home from the hospital in Inuvik. I told my mother I was in good shape, but Ryan had to get sewn up a little. She had me on speaker. My cousin Billy got all excited when I explained that Ryan had a run-in with the grolar bear. Billy wanted to know all about it. I told him it was a long story. "Jonah wants to see you really bad," Billy said.

"Tell him I can't wait," I said. "We've got some pictures to show him."

"Lots of caribou?"

"Oh, yeah."

My mother said that the Royal Canadian Air Force sent a plane to take a look at Shingle Point. They were reporting that 40 percent of the plywood cabins had been swept away, and most of the rest had taken heavy damage. "Sounds like we'll have to rebuild, Nick."

"This summer, I hope."

My mom asked if I was going to bring my brother home to meet everybody. "Tomorrow," I told her. She asked if she should pick us up at the Mackenzie River ferry with the motorboat. "No," I said, "Red Wiley is going to fly us home free of charge."

There's not much more to tell. I met up with Jonah right where I left him, at home in his recliner. "So happy to see you, Nick," was the first thing he said. And the second was, "Billy says you saw lots of caribou."

That put a big smile on my face. "More than lots, Grampa."

"That's good to hear. That's just what I was hoping. You must have quite a story to tell."

"Do I ever. I'll be back to tell it after you rest up."

He looked doubtful about that idea.

"Grandma said you should rest," I told him.

"Well then, okay."

"It'll be better with Ryan here. He's getting cleaned up right now. Then it's my turn."

"The bear and the wolf are at the edge of town. You hurry back."

"You better believe I will," I promised.

A couple hours later the whole family gathered at my grandparents'. Jonah was alert as can be, watching Ryan's slide show on my laptop as I sat by his side and told our story. Jonah's eyes went wide at me telling of the raft flipping over and me and Ryan finding ourselves under the ice. He looked to my brother for an explanation. Ryan smiled and shrugged, and said, "I guess there's a first time for everything."

Jonah chuckled. I could tell he had liked Ryan from the moment he walked through the door.

The pictures Jonah enjoyed the most—no surprise— were the ones Ryan took of the immense caribou gathering on the upper Trail River. Jonah wanted to see those over and over. "My, my," he kept saying. "That's what it was like, all those years ago." He put his hand over mine and rested it there.

Two days later Jonah died in his sleep. The weekend after his funeral, people came from far and wide to remember him. The community hall was packed. There was throat singing and drum dancing and fiddle music and tables full of food, most of it from the river and the land and the ocean.

That night Ryan gave his slide show to a packed house. People wanted to see pictures of caribou, and did they ever! It was a celebration of our land that did everybody proud.

People took to Ryan in a big way. And to think how afraid I had been, only weeks before, of him even showing up in Aklavik.

I wish Jonah had lived long enough to see that issue of *National Geographic*. The cover story was Ryan's "Change Comes to the Arctic." The cover photo was of the grolar bear at the Last Mountain campsite, standing at the edge of the Firth River. Even without a human arm in its jaws, the strangeness of the creature and the look in its eye jumped out at you.

The article ended with Ryan reporting the results of the new 2010 census of the Porcupine caribou herd, and the relief that washed over Aklavik when we heard the amazing news. The aerial survey had counted 170,000 caribou, up from 120,000 in 2001. "Why the Porcupine herd was rebounding while the Bathurst herd to the east was collapsing," Ryan wrote, "has the caribou biologists scratching their heads and calling for further study. On the street in Aklavik, people say that's the way it's always been—boom and bust—and trust that they and the caribou will survive whatever their warming climate throws at them next."

Ryan stayed with us for three weeks, and helped us rebuild at Shingle Point. He cleaned a whole lot of fish and even tried some muktuk. I think he liked the experience of chewing blubber better than the taste. My brother took a lot of colorful pictures out there. My favorites were of the fish racks, bright red with drying char, and the ones of a fifteen-foot, milky white beluga whale being butchered.

Ryan talked to the elders and he talked to the young people. Lots of people wanted to feed him. He claimed he gained ten pounds.

The morning before Ryan flew back to Inuvik to collect his truck, he took the picture of me in front of Moose Kerr School, the one on the article's last page. I'm pointing to Aklavik's motto, NEVER SAY DIE.

We keep in touch by email. Ryan hopes I'll go to college instead of working in the diamond mines or on the offshore rigs if and when the big oil companies start drilling in the Beaufort Sea. He offered to teach me how to do landscape and wildlife photography. He says there will be a huge demand for photographs from the changing North, especially from an Inuit photographer.

Truth be told, I got hooked when I first turned through the pages of Ryan's article and saw a photograph of three magnificent caribou bulls fording the Trail River. In the background, an ocean of caribou is lapping against the mountains. Hey, I thought, I took that picture.

A closer look, and I noticed lettering in small print alongside the photograph. NICK THRASHER, it said. Jonah would have liked that.